Heavy Metal

HEAVY METAL

ANDREW BOURELLE

Autumn House Press

Pittsburgh

"Autumn House Press" and "Autumn House" are registered trademarks owned by Autumn House Press, a nonprofit corporation whose mission is the publication and promotion of poetry and other fine literature.

Autumn House Press receives state arts funding support through a grant from the Pennsylvania Council on the Arts, a state agency funded by the Commonwealth of Pennsylvania, and the National Endowment for the Arts, a federal agency.

ISBN: 978-1-938769-19-1

Library of Congress Control Number: 2016955597

All Autumn House books are printed on acid-free paper and meet the international standards of permanent books intended for purchase by libraries.

For Ed

I place the gun barrel between my lips, touch the roof of my mouth with the sight, test the hardness of the steel with my teeth. I pull it out, put it back, pull it out again. I cock the hammer back, uncock it. It's a .44 Magnum. I press my finger against the polished steel, and, when I pull it back, my fingerprint is momentarily recorded on the metal, white lines in a circular whirlpool. And then the lines disappear. I place the gun against my temple. Under my chin. Back in my mouth.

That's how Mom did it. Through the mouth. When I found her, the top of her head was opened up, with pieces of skull, big concave chunks of bone, folded out like wedges of a smashed pumpkin. Her hair was matted and sticky. The inside of the hole was red and gooey, like strawberry jam only darker, with little white flakes like pieces of eggshell.

When I hear the front door open, I hide the gun behind my back in the recliner, pick up the remote, and un-mute the TV. The video for Ozzy Osbourne's "Crazy Train" is starting.

My brother stomps in. His jean jacket is wet, but he doesn't take it off. His face is damp, his black hair shiny like a crow's feathers. His jacket is unbuttoned, and underneath is his Iron Maiden concert shirt, with a picture of Eddie, the ghoulish creature from all the band's album covers, floating above an icy sea and holding in its hand an unborn monstrous version of itself struggling in a placental sack, a red umbilical rope still connecting the two creatures.

Craig grabs the phone from the stand and drags the cord across the room to sit down on the couch. He punches numbers and waits.

Where's Dad? he asks me.

Passed out.

In bed?

Yeah.

How'd he—He stops and talks into the phone. Hello. Is Gretchen there?

I mute the TV and hear a muffled voice on the other end. A woman's voice, asking who this is and does he know what time it is.

This is Craig. Is Gretchen there?

I hear the woman say, She said she had a date. I thought she was with you.

No, he says. She is *not* with me.

The voice on the other end is more muffled and I can't make out what she says.

Tell her I called.

I hear the woman say, I'm going back to sleep.

Craig rolls his eyes, raises his voice. Well, then tell her in the morning.

He slams the phone down and stares at the TV.

You gonna un-mute that?

I press the button, and we hear Ozzy singing.

Is this *Headbangers Ball*?

Yeah.

Is it that late?

Dad's watch is lying on the coffee table next to his ashtray and empty cans. I lean forward and look at it, then lean back quickly to cover the gun.

It's ten till one.

He looks at the couch he's sitting on and turns to me. His eyes are red, like he's stoned or been crying.

You help him get to bed? he asks.

Carried him.

By yourself?

I nod.

He looks at me, his eyes going up from my shoes to the top of my head. And then his eyes keep traveling upward, as if he's seeing my future growth.

I guess you're getting bigger.

I look away from him to the TV. A Def Leppard video comes on.

You're gonna be as big as me soon.

Bigger, I say, and grin.

We'll see about that, he says, standing up. I'm gonna go looking for Gretchen. You want to come?

Sure.

Well, get your jacket and let's go.

He turns toward Dad's gun cabinet and I rise slowly, trying to tuck the pistol in the back of my jeans. The barrel is too long, so it doesn't work like it does for cops in movies. I back toward the kitchen. I lay the gun silently on top of the refrigerator, and grab my jacket off the back of the chair. Walking back to the TV room, I see Craig crouched, looking through the bottom panel of the case, beneath the rifles and shotguns.

Where's Dad's pistol?

I don't know.

He keeps searching. It was here the other day.

Maybe he's got it in his room.

He looks at me. The expression on his face tells me he's thinking, weighing how bad he wants the gun versus how bad he doesn't want to go into Dad's room to get it.

He stands and walks down the hall. I wait a few seconds, go to the kitchen and grab the gun and walk after him.

He's in Dad's room. The light from the hall is the only light, and he can't see much. But he's looking on top of Dad's dresser. Dad's snoring, lying face up on the covers, still wearing his blue work shirt, his work boots pointed toward the ceiling.

Hey, I whisper.

Craig looks at me.

I found it.

He comes and closes the door behind him. I hold the gun out to him. He takes it, lifts his hand up and down, the gun in his palm, as if to get a sense of its weight.

It's always heavier than I remember, he says.

Yeah. It isn't like the toys we used to play with.

Is it loaded?

I don't know.

He opens the cylinder to see the six empty holes.

He heads back to the TV room, and I follow. Now a commercial is playing, and I turn the TV off. Craig kneels on the floor, like he's going to pray, and pulls out a box of ammunition. He plugs a cartridge into each empty slot. He works slowly and deliberately, as if thinking about each bullet. He rises, takes the box of shells and tucks it into his jean jacket pocket. He sucks his stomach in and tries to tuck the pistol into his belt. It's too big. He pulls it out, and holds it at his side, his finger outside the trigger guard.

The gun is fourteen inches long from grip to front sight, the barrel eight inches. Empty, the gun weighs four pounds. Loaded with six bullets, I imagine the weight increases exponentially. I imagine each bullet multiplies the weight by a power of two, as if they carry something else—the weight of the future.

Craig lifts the Magnum and gestures with it toward the door as if the gun weighs nothing at all.

Let's go, bro.

The rain has stopped, but the streets are wet. The front walk is slick with the water starting to turn to ice. I see my breath. Inside the Nova, the vinyl seats are cold. Craig sets the gun down on the seat between us. The barrel is pointing at my leg. I don't move it. Craig turns the key and revs the engine. He backs into the street and stomps the gas, squealing the tires. The street here is streaked with black tire scars because he does this so often.

He turns on the cassette player, and Metallica's album *Ride the Lightning* is playing. We listen without speaking. The streets are empty as we head to town, deserted in the early morning. The sky is gray and lit up somehow, as if the foggy clouds glow with a low pulse of electricity. It's not day; it's not night. It's some new time where the sun is gone and we can see as if light exists somehow without a source.

In town, street lights from the BP and the Taco Bell glow, but still no cars drive around, as if the human race has vanished.

The IGA sign is dark. Two cars are parked in the lot, parallel but facing opposite directions, with figures standing around and leaning on the hoods. Craig turns into the lot.

Put that in the glove box, would you?

I pick up the Magnum, feel its weight, its rubber sandpaper grip on my palm.

Here, he says, handing me the box of shells. That too.

I put them inside among his heavy metal tapes and discarded cans of Kodiak.

He cuts the engine and steps out of the car.

Hey, Craig, someone says.

I recognize the faces, but they're mostly seniors, like Craig. One girl is in my Algebra class, a sophomore taking it for the second time. On the first day of school, I sat next to her and she smiled and said hi and I thought maybe we'd become friends, but we've never talked since.

Hey, she says to me.

Hi.

She wears an acid-wash jean jacket and smokes a cigarette. Her front teeth are a little crooked, and she wears pink lipstick. She has pretty green eyes I noticed the first day of school. I think her name is Beth.

I didn't know you were Craig's brother, she says.

Yeah.

I can see it now. You look exactly alike.

Do we?

You're so different, she says. I mean, personality-wise.

Really?

Well, you're just so quiet.

Craig is chatting with the others. Someone hands him beer.

You got one for my kid brother? he asks.

Someone leans into the open door of his car, comes out with a beer, and tosses it to me. Busch Light. I open it and foam comes up like the volcano Mom and I made for science class when I was a kid. Baking soda and vinegar, and when we wanted the foam to be red, we added food coloring. The beer is beginning to get warm. I feel a numbness pour through my limbs.

I smile. Beth laughs at me.

I'm quiet and take another drink.

I like your shirt, she says.

I look down, opening my jacket wider for her to see. It's my Judas Priest tee shirt.

Did you go to that concert?

No. Craig did. He got this for me.

Wow. Nice brother.

She unbuttons her jacket and opens it up. She's wearing an AC/DC shirt, one with Brian Johnson holding Angus Young in the air, his guitar hoisted high.

This was my first concert, she says.

She has large breasts; they push against the fabric.

We should trade shirts sometime, she says.

I don't think yours would fit me, would it?

Okay, well you can just let me borrow yours sometime.

Sure.

We're quiet for a moment.

Hey, Beth, someone asks. You seen Gretchen?

She starts talking with Craig and the rest of the group. I stand and watch. No one has seen Gretchen, but they've heard some people are down at the river.

Maybe we should all go check it out, someone says.

Craig and the others talk. One couple doesn't want to go, so that means five people will be smashed into a Toyota Corolla.

I'll ride with these guys, Beth says, gesturing to Craig and me.

Uh, I have to stop somewhere first, Craig says. Maybe you should go ahead and go with them.

Fine, she says, feigning irritation. Although maybe she is a little hurt.

The five of them—three girls and two guys—climb into the car, with Beth sandwiched in the back between the other two girls. Craig and I get into the Nova and follow the other car toward the exit. The Toyota turns right, and Craig turns left. As we pull across the intersection, I watch the rear lights of the other car driving away.

Sorry, bro, he says.

For what?

He doesn't answer. He pulls into the BP and parks. The store is empty inside, except for the person behind the counter.

Do me a favor, Craig says. He pulls out his wallet from inside his jacket and hands me a ten-dollar bill. Go in there and exchange this for a roll of quarters.

Why?

'Cause the gun's a last resort.

I look at him without moving.

Tell the guy you're going to play video games.

I set my beer down on the floorboard, take the money, and step out of the car. I lean back down to look at Craig.

There's no place with video games that's open this late.

Jesus Christ. Just get the fucking quarters, would you?

After the gas station, he drives to Gretchen's apartment complex. He stops in the parking lot and waits, the engine idling, "Fade to Black" playing quietly. The light above her front door is on, waiting for her to come home. Otherwise, the windows are dark. The parking lot is still. No movement, not even a breeze. An overturned tricycle lies in the sidewalk in front of another apartment. A grill lies on its side, its ashes and half-burned chunks of charcoal spilled on the grass. A window is boarded up, and on the plywood someone has spray-painted an anarchy symbol in red.

A car pulls into the parking lot, and Craig and I both turn to watch. It's a Trans Am, and a twenty-something man with a moustache gets out, carrying a twelve-pack of Milwaukee's Best.

We going to the river or what? I ask.

Sure, he says, and starts the engine. Why not?

He pulls onto a dirt road that leads into forest. The trees hanging over in a canopy hide the light from the gray clouds, and all we can see are ruts in the mud in front of us. Craig drives slowly, unable to see more than a few feet. Branches reach and scrape against the car like skeletal hands.

The trees open up, and the path descends down toward the edge of the river. Two cars are parked—the Toyota and a red Chevy pickup—and a group of people stand around a fire burning in a fifty-gallon drum. Beth and the others from her car are there, along with two guys and another girl. I don't see Gretchen.

It's about time, Beth says, exhaling smoke and tossing her cigarette into the fire. What happened? You guys get lost?

She walks over and hugs me. She smells of hairspray and cigarette smoke, and my legs are shaky. It must be the alcohol, but I accept another beer when someone hands me one. The door of the pickup is open, and the radio is playing pop music I don't recognize.

You guys seen Gretchen? Craig asks the two guys who must have come in the truck, other faces without names from the halls of high school.

She was here earlier, one of them says. He has a buzz haircut and wears a Chicago Bulls jacket.

Yeah?

She left a while ago. She was here with Jamie Fergus.

Craig stares quietly at the fire. The wood is damp, so they've spread branches over the top of the drum to dry. The rusty barrel is punctured with bullet holes, and tongues of flame lick at the openings.

Jamie Fergus the football player? I ask.

You know of another one? Buzzcut says.

Hey, that's my brother you're talking to.

Craig's face glows from the fire, orange like a jack-o-lantern.

Sorry, the guy says. He turns to me. I am his height, and we look eye to eye. What grade you in, kid?

Freshman.

Yeah? I haven't seen you around school.

I seen him, the guy he's with says, then turns to me. I didn't know you two was brothers, but I seen you.

He has a face full of acne and a varsity jacket, with a black "T" for our town and a "90" for the year he'll graduate.

The others, Beth's friends, introduce themselves now. Angie, who has short black hair, is a cheerleader I recognize. Danielle wears a leather jacket and red cowboy boots. Dawn's jean jacket is covered in buttons with kitschy sayings. A cigarette is tucked behind her ear like a pencil. The boys from Beth's car are Luke and Doug, friends of Craig's I've seen before, with long hair and stubble, concert tee shirts and jean jackets. The two guys from the pickup truck are Larry and Dave.

Dave, the one with the acne, looks at Craig. I thought you and Gretchen broke up.

We broke up a million times. We always get back together.

Silence for several seconds, and then Beth grabs my arm. This fire's too hot. Come over here with me, Danny.

We walk away from the fire, and the temperature drops with every step. At the bank, we look out at the river. The water is black, like motor oil, flowing along slowly. Light from the fire reflects off the current. I pick up a rock and skip it across the water, and the light catches the splashes as if each bounce elicits sparks of electricity.

We talk about Algebra and how she's failing again and how I could tutor her and that it's not so hard it's just that the teacher sucks. She smiles and she smokes and I feel the beer going through me and I think that my blood must be like the river and that the beer is like the embers of light riding along on its surface. I heard somewhere that blood is not red until it comes out of your body and I think that doesn't make much sense but maybe it's black because water isn't clear until the light hits it. I think about how maybe Beth could be my girlfriend like Gretchen was to Craig and then maybe I wouldn't have to stay at home on Saturday nights watching *Headbangers Ball* and playing with Dad's gun wondering what death is like and if everything just goes black like in the Metallica song.

I think I'm a little drunk, I say to Beth, and we both start laughing.

Hey, Danny, my brother calls. I got an idea.

He asks me to start setting empty beer bottles and cans on a log lying on the bank. I help him. No one knows what we're doing but I do.

After we've set up ten or twelve bottles and cans, Craig walks to the Nova and comes back with the Magnum.

Whoa! the guy with the acne says. Look at that cannon.

That's a goddamn Dirty Harry gun, someone says.

Everyone gathers behind Craig back by the fire, about twenty feet from the log. He raises the gun with both hands and points it toward the targets, the glass and aluminum illuminated in front of the black, sparkling current of the river. Embers from the fire float toward the river like fireflies and disappear in the darkness.

I lean close to Beth, gesturing with my hands. Cover your ears, I whisper.

Craig concentrates for several seconds. Fire explodes from the barrel, and a spout of water shoots up from the river.

Damn, Craig says, looking at the gun. I missed.

Holy shit! Buzzcut says, fanning his hand in front of him to clear the smoke. My ears are ringing.

Beth smiles at me.

Craig aims again, this time for only a couple seconds, and shoots again, the sound like thunder through the trees. He misses the bottle, and there's another spray of water.

Shit, Craig says, stepping forward. I'm getting closer.

Give me that thing, I say, holding out my hand.

Go ahead. Try to do better.

Now everyone is watching me. I cock the hammer back with my thumb. I lift the gun with one hand, align the sights, and squeeze the trigger slowly. When the gun goes off, it's a surprise. The barrel kicks upward, and an MGD bottle explodes with enough force that it knocks over a bottle next to it. A spout of water erupts in the river behind. My ears change, and now every sound is muffled through a constant high-pitched tone.

I guess he did show you, Angie says.

Craig laughs.

Christ, that's the loudest thing I've ever heard, Luke says.

I fire off three more shots in quick succession. The first launches a can backward into the river, the second misses and splashes into the water, and the third disintegrates another empty bottle.

What's wrong with you? Buzzcut says. You missed one.

Everyone is laughing and asking to shoot. I take the box of ammunition from Craig and begin to reload. The air smells of gunpowder.

Where'd you learn to shoot like that? Craig asks.

Sometimes when Dad works Saturdays I take the gun into the woods.

You little son of…. He trails off, shaking his head, grinning. Doesn't Dad miss the ammo?

I stole a bunch from the Wal-Mart, I say.

I close the cylinder—it's hot to the touch—and offer the gun to Beth. Want to try?

Wow. It's heavy, she says.

We play this way for a while, with each person taking a turn. Most can't hit anything, and the group moves forward so they don't have to shoot as far. Craig takes the gun back and blasts holes into the fire barrel. Each shot opens an eyehole with fire blinking out, and the metal drum shakes and rings like a muffled church bell. We drink more, and when the box of shells is almost empty, I tell them that I want to try something. I ask Beth to toss a bottle up into the air so I can try to shoot it before it hits the ground.

No way you can do it, Doug says. Not shooting from the hip.

Beth throws a bottle of Budweiser up and I miss it, the shot going out into the darkness, and the bottle splashes into the water near the shore and begins to float away on the current. I shoot it as it floats, and it disappears in an explosion of water.

Try again, Beth says, prying a half-sunk whiskey bottle out of the soil.

I cock the hammer back, hold the gun at my side like a gunslinger. She tosses the bottle high, and it seems to float down as if it's a leaf. I have plenty of time. The glass explodes like a bottle rocket, the shards glinting in the firelight underneath the gray-lit sky.

Everyone applauds and smiles. Craig smiles too, sitting on the hood of the car with an expression that actually looks like happiness.

He hops down and takes the gun from me, puts the last few cartridges in the cylinder, and turns to put the gun back in the car. For a few seconds he is preoccupied inside the Nova. He calls out, Hey, Larry, turn that shit off. Let's listen to some real music.

The tolling gong from the opening of AC/DC's "Hells Bells" comes out of the Nova's speakers.

Yeah! Beth shouts.

She opens her jacket to show off her tee shirt, tilting her head back and dancing around in circles. I smile and wonder how long it's been since I felt so happy.

Beth and I lie on a blanket she borrowed from one of her friends. We're next to the river, the water lapping near our feet. I stare up into the sky, looking at the trees arching over my vision. It's cold, and Beth is snuggled against me. The music is still playing and the others are still drinking. I feel like time has stopped and this night will never end. Already it seems like we've been out long enough for dawn to have come and gone. But the world is still covered in a gray-mist sky. I'm hoping Beth will kiss me.

That gun was so powerful, Beth says. I think my ears have finally stopped ringing.

Mine too.

Have you ever shot anything with it? I mean, like a living thing?

My dad shot a cat once, I say. It almost blew it in half.

Gross.

Its guts were splattered five feet.

Whose cat was it?

I don't know. Dad said it was a stray, but it had a collar.

That's terrible, she says, sitting up and looking down at me. I cock my head so I can see her.

Well, that's my dad, I say.

Imagine what that gun would do to a person, she says, staring off toward the river.

Actually, I say, that's the gun my mom used to kill herself.

Beth gasps. Oh my god. I'm so sorry. I forgot. I mean, I knew Craig's mom…I guess I just forgot you two were brothers.

It's okay.

I can't believe I touched it, she says, looking at her hands. I can't believe you….

It's just a piece of metal, I say, even though I don't believe it. The trigger doesn't pull itself.

She touches my arm and looks at me intensely, as if trying to see inside of me. She opens her mouth to speak, but then closes it. She doesn't know what to say.

I found her, I say. After I got home from school.

Beth inhales deeply as if the wind's been knocked out of her. That must have been awful.

There was a lot of blood, I say, looking out at the black water. More than you'd think a human body could fit inside it. It was like someone had hosed the room down, spraying it up on the wall, on the ceiling.

I turn to Beth, and her eyes are filled with tears. I can't believe I'm saying what I'm saying, but I guess it's the alcohol.

Sorry, I say. I don't usually talk about it.

It's okay, she says, and she leans forward and hugs me. I pause for a moment, and I let myself be comforted. I hold her and smell her and find a safety in her that I haven't felt in a long time.

I hear a car engine, and then headlights glide over us. A new car pulls down into the clearing. It sits, engine rumbling, and I can't see inside because of the headlights.

Hey, motherfucker! Craig shouts and starts toward the car.

Oh, shit, Beth says. That's Jamie Fergus's Camaro.

I stand and hurry toward the fire.

A man steps out of the driver's side and stands looking at my brother. He's as tall as Craig but broader in the shoulders. His varsity jacket is tight like it's a size too small. Gretchen jumps out of the other side and hurries around the car, her curly blonde hair bouncing. She is very pretty, but she was never nice to me.

Craig, what the hell are you doing?

Stay out of this.

No, Jamie says, you stay out of this.

Jamie pushes Craig in the chest, and he stumbles backward, his dexterity off because he's drunk. He goes down on one knee. He looks like he's trying to get his balance, and he reaches into his jacket pocket. For a moment, I think he's going to pull out the gun, but that's impossible; it couldn't fit in his pocket. Instead, his hand comes out clenched in a fist. He jumps and rushes toward Jamie. He swings and connects with Jamie's cheekbone, and coins burst out of his fist, shining in the firelight like a spray of water. Jamie's head whips back, his butt hits the fender of his Camaro, and his body rolls sideways on the edge of the hood and flops on the ground. The quarters sparkle in the dirt.

What the hell was that? someone says.

You cocksucker! Gretchen screams at Craig.

Fuck you, you slut!

They yell at each other, Craig leaning over her, Jamie at their feet as still as my passed-out Dad. Craig's face is red, veins standing out on his neck like snakes slithering under his skin.

I watch from a few steps back with the rest of the group. Beth clings to my arm.

Gretchen starts to swing her fists at him, and he swats them away. She lunges at him with her hands clawed, going toward his face with her nails, and he pushes her back.

I fucking hate you! she screams, her face twisted and crying. You were the biggest mistake I ever made.

Oh, yeah?

He stomps off toward the Nova.

No, Craig, Beth whispers.

He comes back carrying the pistol at his side. With the stainless steel shining, it looks more like a long knife.

He lifts it and points it at her, and I step between the gun and Gretchen.

Danny, he says, voice trembling. Get out of the way.

No.

Danny! Get the fuck out of the way!

Can't let you do it, bro.

The barrel is two feet from my face. The hole under the front sight looks enormous, like I could fit a finger in it, a thumb. The bullet would pass through my brain before I even see fire spit from the barrel.

Go ahead and shoot me, I say.

I'll fucking do it.

Go ahead.

He cocks the hammer back and moves his finger from outside the trigger guard to inside.

Go ahead and do it! I yell.

Danny—

You're the only one who gives a shit about me and you're pointing a gun to my head! What do I have to live for? Go ahead and fucking shoot!

I step closer and jut my head forward, pressing the hole at the end of the gun to my forehead. I stare at his finger on the trigger.

Shoot me! Fucking shoot me!

And then I scream without words, just a guttural, primal noise, until he pulls the gun away.

His face is pale like a skull, with deep black sockets swallowing his eyes. He turns and runs to the car, revving the engine and kicking up dirt and gravel as he spins the car in a one-eighty and accelerates up the embankment and into the woods. Beth is at my side, wiping my tears. The others are around me, talking, but I can't hear them. Noise is muffled as if my ears are still ringing but they aren't. I'm only able to look at Beth and breathe in and out, pulling her into me with each inhalation.

Gretchen and the others rouse Jamie from unconsciousness. His cheekbone is red and already swelling, the white of the eye turning bloodshot. He sits upright but does not stand, groggy, as if coming out of anesthesia. They help him into the passenger seat, and Gretchen drives his car away without speaking to me or looking at me.

We stay a while longer, the others so full of adrenaline from what happened that they can't stop talking about it, replaying how they saw it from their respective angles. Danielle crawls on her hands and knees and searches for the quarters, but she only finds seven dollars and fifty cents worth. Beth holds my hand, and we watch the fire die, diminishing from flames to just red flickering coals. The mood becomes subdued as exhaustion settles over everyone, and people begin describing what they see in the coals. Like a sky of red clouds at sunset, the embers make shapes. One person sees a bear, another a horse. One girl says she sees her grandmother in her rocking chair.

I don't tell the others I see faces. Faces with open, screaming mouths, faces with elongated mutant eye sockets. Faces rupturing from wounds, spilling pink foamy blood like the homemade volcanoes Mom and I made for third-grade science class.

When the Toyota pulls into my driveway, Craig's Nova is there, parked askew with one wheel in the grass. Beth walks me to the door.

Call me tomorrow, she says. Or...I guess I mean today.

The horizon to the east glows golden.

I will, I say.

Promise?

I promise.

She leans in to kiss me, and I kiss her back clumsily. Her tongue stretches into my mouth, burning me from my throat to my chest, and the warmth emanates to my limbs. My black blood lights up and brightens like the sunrise.

Craig is passed out on the couch, where Dad usually sleeps. The Magnum is on the floor next to him. I look at Craig closely. His chest barely rises and falls. He looks younger than I think he should. I always think of him as a man, but seeing him asleep, his face relaxed, he looks like a little boy, like he's younger than me.

I walk down the hall to Dad's room and stand at his feet. The dawn is coming in through the window, bringing light to the darkness like a developing Polaroid picture. He is still in the same position, face toward the ceiling, snoring silently. He used to be as big as Craig, but now he is gaunt, like he's rotting from the inside.

Back to the living room, I pick up the gun and check to see if it's still loaded. It is. The box of shells is on the couch, wedged between Craig's body and a cushion. I pull the box out. Craig doesn't wake up. The box is mashed and malformed and empty. Dad will notice all of this. I pull the bullets out one by one and place them back in the box. Each one looks like a missile, and I know that's what they are because I have seen what they can do. They can blow up bottles and cans and cats, but they can blow up whole worlds too.

It happened last spring. The weather had just broken. It was a nice warm day. Dad was working. Craig was with Gretchen at the mall. I'd gone for a walk in the woods near the house. I think sometimes that I should have heard the shot. I wasn't far from home. I imagine a moment where I hear it, the distant, muffled crack of Dad's gun. I know what has happened and I come running.

But it wasn't that way. I never heard anything. I was walking around the woods, breathing in the air, enjoying the peace and the solitude. I was taking a break from doing my homework back when stuff like that mattered. I was out there—happy—and she was already dead. I'll never forgive myself for that.

I awaken with a start, as if I've been slapped or a loud noise startled me. One second I'm asleep, in darkness so complete it feels like a coma, and then my eyes are wide and I'm trying to recall if everything that happened last night was real or a dream. I hear the faint noise of the TV down the hall and nothing else.

I sit up. The room is cold. I put on sweatpants and a sweatshirt and walk barefoot down the hall. As I turn the corner to the living room, I expect, as I always do, to see Mom sitting on the couch, curled in a blanket, with both hands around a mug of coffee. My heart aches. I wonder when I'll stop expecting to see her.

What the hell you doing sleeping so late? Dad says.

He's watching a football game and drinking a beer and smoking a cigarette. He doesn't look up at me.

Just tired, I say.

I go to the kitchen and pour myself a bowl of Cheerios. The tile is cold on my feet.

I need you to wash my work clothes, he calls from the other room.

Okay.

Shit, he says.

What?

Goddamn interception.

Oh.

I carry the bowl and eat as I walk. I try to look out the front door but can't see through the layer of perspiration on the window. I wipe the moisture away with my hand. Craig's parking spot sits empty. The Nova is so loud it normally wakes me up, if I'm not already awake. Not today. It feels as if time has skipped forward somehow. The sleep I had was deep and long, and the world moved on without me.

I rinse my bowl and put it and the rest of the dirty dishes into the dishwasher, and I head back toward my room and stop on my way and ask Dad where Craig is.

Work, I guess, he says. Or with what's her name.

He doesn't look up from the game. With his beer in one hand, his cigarette in the fingers of the other, his body is tensed as if it's a coiled spring that, at any point, might jump from the chair.

He drinks his beer and pulls on his cigarette and exhales through his nostrils, the lines of smoke like a pressure release on a steam engine ready to boil over.

A commercial comes on, and he notices me watching him. He says, almost nicely, You want something, Son?

No.

I go to Dad's room, gather up his work clothes—jeans and dark blue shirts with his name on a patch over the breast—and I put them into the washing machine.

I wonder if I should call Beth yet, but I decide it might be too early since she went to bed just as late as I did. My clothes from the night before smell like campfire smoke, and I pull my hair around in front of my nose and it smells too. I can't take a shower because Dad's clothes are in the wash. So I put on a clean pair of jeans, a flannel shirt, and my jacket, which still smells of campfire smoke too, and I tell my dad I'm going out for a while.

Where? he says.

Just out, I say. I'll put your clothes in the dryer when I get back.

This answer is good enough because he doesn't look up from the TV.

The air is cold, and the breeze blows my hair back from my forehead as I walk down the highway toward the truck-stop diner where Craig works. It's two miles by road, but I cut through an empty field. The ground is frozen, and the clumps of dirt are uneven, making the trek awkward and unsteady. The earth crunches under my feet. Broken cornstalks lay scattered like bones. Dark clouds loom overhead like rocky upside-down mountains. I shove my hands in my pockets and as much as I try to think about Craig and worry about him, I mostly think about Beth. I suppose this is what it means to be falling for someone.

When I push through the door into the restaurant, warm air surrounds me. I clench and unclench my fists.

Hey, Danny, Cheryl says.

The lunch rush is over, and she is the only waitress on duty, carrying a pot of coffee back from the only customer in the place. She's older than my dad and has a voice like she's smoked since she was my age.

Hi, I say. Is Craig here?

He's in the kitchen. Go on back if you want.

Craig is washing dishes, wearing a big maroon apron and blasting the plates clean with a spray hose.

Hey, bro, I say.

He looks up. Oh, he says. Hey.

He lets go of the nozzle and it bounces around on its spring-loaded carrier. He takes off the apron and hangs it on a hook next to the dishwasher and leans next to the machine.

What's going on? he says.

Nothing, I say.

Now that I'm here I don't know what to say.

Want something to eat?

I shrug.

He cooks me a burger, and while it fries on the grill, we don't talk. Then, once the food is in front of me and I'm sitting at a metal table with my plate next to the aluminum foil and plastic wrap and industrial-sized can opener, he says, I'm sorry about last night, bro.

Me too.

You got nothing to be sorry for.

I'm just sorry all that happened, I say.

Well, I want you to know that I'd never hurt you.

I know.

I pop a french fry into my mouth. We hear the bell rattle as someone walks in the front door, and Craig peeks out through the pickup window to make sure it isn't the owner. I poise myself, ready to dump my food into the trash and put the dish with the dirty plates in the sink, but Craig looks at me and shakes his head. Just a regular customer.

I'll tell you one thing, Craig says.

What's that?

It's a good thing we're slow today because I'm hungover as hell.

I smile, and he tells me about one time when he had to work the breakfast shift after drinking too much. He was sweating like he was sitting in a sauna, leaning over the grill full of eggs and bacon and pancakes. He puked into the garbage can and Cheryl came running back, telling him she could hear him out front.

I guess I'm like Dad, he says. I always make it to work no matter how miserable I am.

He sits quietly for several seconds, and he seems really sad. I feel like I can read his mind. He's thinking about how he doesn't like to see Dad's traits in himself.

Do you think you're more like Mom or you're more like Dad? he says.

I was about to take another bite of the hamburger, but I put it down. I look at the pink in the center of the meat and my appetite is gone.

I don't know, I say.

I think you got the best parts of both.

I smile.

Craig is good at saying these types of things to me, and I want to say good things back. His girlfriend just broke up with him and he got in a fight and he's hurting bad enough to do what he did last night, and I feel like I should say something to him. I don't think it's fair that just because he's the big brother that the burden of being the strong one should always fall on him.

Cheryl puts an order on the wheel, spins it, and rings the bell to let Craig know it's there even though both of us are watching her. He walks over and pulls off the ticket and sticks it up over the grill and starts working on the meal. I watch him in a sort of hypnotic trance, realizing that our conversation about serious stuff is over. I missed my chance.

He slaps a hamburger patty on the grill and it begins to sizzle. He pours a generous portion of frozen french fries into the wire basket and plops the basket down into the grease. The grease bubbles loudly, and Craig presses a button on the timer.

So what happened with you and that girl Beth last night? he says. You gonna ask her out?

He picks up a spatula and slides it across the grill like he's sharpening a knife on a stone. The air smells of frying beef.

She kissed me, I say, and I can't help but grin as I say it.

He turns, smiling genuinely.

All right! he shouts.

I'm sure he knows it's my first kiss and I'm prepared for him to tease me about it and press me for details, but he doesn't.

We talk more, and when I tell him that I'm supposed to call her today, he says, What the hell are you waiting for, Danny? Go use the phone in the office.

The office is a small room with a window in the door that looks out into the kitchen. It has a desk and a chair and a mounted deer head hanging above a calendar featuring a scenic photograph of a cascading waterfall. The month is wrong. No one bothered to flip the page. I sit at the desk and look at the phone. I pull the piece of paper with Beth's phone number out of my pocket and look at it. The paper is wrinkled. I smooth it. She wrote her name and number and drew a large heart around them.

It's a rotary phone, and I dial the first number and have to wait as the circle spins back to true before I'm able to dial the next number. The next digit is a nine and the wait feels like minutes. Then another nine. And I forget if I've dialed both nines and I nervously hang up and start over.

When I redial and the phone finally rings, I'm tempted to hang up again.

But then there's a voice on the other end. I think it's her, but I can't be sure.

Hi, is Beth there?

This is Beth, she says, and I'm sure she knows it's me but she's waiting.

Hi, it's Danny, I say, and it's out there: I've called her.

Hi! she says.

Relief washes over me like the buzz from a beer because of the excitement in her voice, and I'm still nervous, but my level of nervousness has been cut in half by the way she said that one word. Not the word itself, just the way she said it.

Beth asks what I'm doing, and I tell her that I'm at McCormack's Restaurant because Craig's working. She asks how he is and if everything is okay between us, and I say that life has returned to normal. It was just a crazy night.

What are you doing? I say, and I lean back in the chair like it's my own office.

I kick my feet forward and relax and listen to Beth. My foot hits something underneath the desk. Down below is a safe, a small one, no bigger than the little cooler Dad takes his lunch to work in. The door, a gunmetal blue color with a combination lock, is ajar. Inside are stacks of cash. Suddenly I'm uncomfortable again, and Beth is talking but I'm not listening because I know I shouldn't be in here. If the owner came in, old man McCormack, Craig would get fired.

I hear silence on the other end of the line and realize that Beth asked me a question.

Uh, could you say that again?

Do you want to come over? she says. You know, just hang out?

Yeah, I say, standing. That'd be great.

I step into the kitchen, and Craig is making hamburger patties. He slaps a glob of red meat back and forth between his hands, then presses it between two plates to flatten it, then lays it atop another patty, divided by a square of wax paper. I watch him as he reaches for another handful of meat, laying it on a scale and weighing it at a quarter pound. He slaps it back and forth between his hands, packing it like a snowball.

So, he says, looking up from his work while his hands continue to move, did you talk to her?

I'm going over there now, I say. To hang out.

Awesome, he says. Beth is a cool girl.

He finishes the patty and picks up a Styrofoam cup off the table. He spits into it. His lower lip bulges from a plug of snuff. He spits again.

I'm sorry about you and Gretchen, I say.

He smirks. Screw it, he says.

I want to change the subject, so I say, There's a shitload of money in that safe, isn't there?

He looks at me. You opened the safe?

I didn't open it. It was already open.

Just sitting there open?

Yeah.

He spits and the oily saliva stretches like a rope into the cup. The rope breaks and he spits again.

That's not normal? I say.

It's always locked as far as I know.

He gets up to go see for himself. I lean against the metal worktable. He comes walking quickly back, his eyes wide.

Holy shit, he says.

He goes back over to the hamburger and finishes the paddy he was working on. He starts a new one. He works quicker now.

I've never seen that much money in one place before, he says.

I didn't think about that, I say.

His excitement is contagious and suddenly I'm excited even though I wasn't before.

How much do you think is there? I say.

He shakes his head, frowns. A few thousand, I guess.

I look out into the dining room, which has only one customer, finishing the hamburger Craig cooked. Cheryl is standing and talking to him, holding a pot of coffee in one hand and a towel in the other.

Money is tight with Mom gone and Dad's is the only income. Maybe Craig is thinking about this, but maybe he isn't. Craig has a job and some money. He might not be thinking about us—me, him, and Dad—but about himself and about how he'll be eighteen soon and out of high school and college isn't a realistic option.

I didn't know this place did enough business to make much profit, I say.

Craig laughs. Neither did I.

I want to leave, to go meet up with Beth, but I'm afraid Craig might do something stupid.

I'm sure they keep a good count of it, I say. It's not like you could take any of it.

He looks at me with an expression that says he knows what I was thinking and he's insulted that I was thinking it.

No shit, he says. I'm not that fucking stupid, Danny.

Out in the cold again, the icy air slithers through the gaps in my clothes, coming in between the buttons of my jacket, knifing its way down past my collar and chilling my skin. Particles of snow float in the air, drifting this way and that like pollen in the breeze. The clouds have changed to gray-fog skies, one solid color from horizon to zenith, with the sun a blob of blurry white trying to bleed through the haze. My breath smokes out of my mouth and nose like car exhaust. Now that I'm already in town, Beth's house—according to her directions—shouldn't be too far away. Maybe another half mile.

The town seems as empty as the restaurant, rarely a car going by. Everyone is staying indoors, warming themselves by fires, watching football, baking cookies, whatever people do.

A police car passes me. Its brake lights flash, then it flips a quick U-turn and pulls up in the gravel breakdown lane next to me.

The window rolls down, powered by an electric motor. The driver is Sergeant Frederickson.

Hey, Danny, he says, and he smiles like he always does when he sees me.

I can never tell if it's fake or sincere.

Hi, Sergeant Frederickson, I say, and I walk over to the car.

My heart always beats hard around cops, even when there's no reason for it. But after last night there's a reason for it, so my heart is really pounding. But he's smiling. He probably wouldn't be if he knew anything about what happened.

You can call me George, Danny.

Right.

It's awful cold for a walk, he says.

I'm okay.

Where you headed?

A friend's house.

You want a ride?

That's okay.

Come on, he says. It's a slow day. I've got time.

A car passes. The driver is a woman with a preteen girl in the passenger seat, and she looks at me, probably wondering what kind of trouble I'm in, a longhaired hood talking to a cop.

I'm going to worry about you out here in the cold, Danny. Let me give you a ride.

The car is warm inside. Sergeant Frederickson wears a pistol—an automatic, not a revolver like my dad's—and a shotgun is strapped in place by his right leg. The radio squeaks static and the dispatcher reports a code of some sort that is meaningless to me.

So how've you been?

Not bad, I say.

I never know what to say to Sergeant Frederickson. He is trying to be nice, but I wish he had left me alone to walk in the cold.

Sergeant Frederickson has close-cropped hair and a mustache, and his chubby cheeks and belly suggest he's out of shape, but I can tell by his arms and his hands that he's strong. He was once very strong and that strength never really leaves. Like my dad, as skinny as he is, the power is still there, condensed somehow. Sergeant Frederickson is the opposite: he's softer, fatter, but underneath the strength is still there too. You can see it in people like them, in their hands, in their arms, even in their eyes, just the way they look.

Staying out of trouble? he says, pulling away from the curb.

The warmth turns to hot, and I want to unbutton my jacket but I don't.

Yeah.

I know you are, he says, looking around as he drives. I worry about your brother and what kind of trouble he might get into, Danny, but I don't worry about you.

I say nothing, and he says nothing more.

Then I tell him to turn, and I pull the paper out of my pocket. I wrote the directions to Beth's house on the back of the same paper with her number. I'm careful not to show Sergeant Frederickson the heart with the phone number inside.

I tell him what street the house is on.

You want me to drop you off a few houses away? he says. So you don't freak your friends out with a cop dropping you off.

That's okay.

You sure? I don't want to hurt your street cred or anything.

I think about it. It's fine, I say. I don't care.

That's my boy, he says.

Silence as the houses slip past.

I think this is it, I say. This one here.

Beth lives in a duplex, the house blue and paint-chipped, the lawn brown from the winter. On the B side, which is the one Beth lives in, a Chevy pickup sits in the driveway, its bed lined with toolboxes and scaffolded with a rack of two-by-fours strapped down with black rubber bungee cords.

Frederickson puts the car in park and lets it idle.

Thanks for the ride.

My pleasure.

I reach for the door.

Danny.

I look at him, and he's serious now.

How's your dad?

He's okay.

Yeah?

Yeah. Working a lot.

And Craig. How's he? Really?

Craig's okay, I say, and I say this in such a way that I want him to know I mean it even if he doesn't believe me about Dad.

I worry about you. If you ever need anything....

I'm okay, I say.

He's just trying to be helpful, but now I'm irritated because there's nothing he can do and so he's just trying to make himself feel better, not actually helping. I'm smart enough to know this, why isn't he?

I gotta go, I say.

I open the door.

Thanks for the ride, Sergeant Frederickson, I say, and I close the door and walk into the cold.

Next to the front door is a window and standing in it are Beth and a man and a woman watching me walk from the police cruiser.

Beth opens the door and welcomes me in, and I turn and Frederickson is waiting to make sure I make it inside. He raises a hand behind the tinted glass, but I turn away without raising mine. I hear the sound of the car driving away. Then the door is shut and Beth is introducing me to her mom and her mom's boyfriend.

What was that all about? her mom's boyfriend says.

Jared, Beth says. Don't be rude.

He just gave me a ride, I say.

Just gave you a ride? the guy says.

He is short and stocky like a bulldog in human form, in a Harley Davidson tee shirt with the sleeves cut off. He has a mustache that looks thinner than some high schoolers' but he must be around forty years old.

Gave you a ride? he says again. No cop ever just gave me a ride.

He's a...

I start to say friend but stop myself.

I know him, I say.

How do you know him? the boyfriend asks.

Jared, Beth says. God. Leave him alone.

What? Some kid I never seen before shows up with a police escort. I can't help but be curious.

Now all of them are looking at me, even Beth, and I know she wants to know too.

I look Jared in the eyes. If I tell him that Sergeant Frederickson was the first cop there when my mom killed herself, his head will jerk back like I slapped him. I am tempted to say this, to make him feel guilty like this—he seems to deserve it—but I don't.

He knows my dad, I say. That's all.

Beth grabs my arm and pulls me toward the hallway. Come on, Danny.

It was nice to meet you, Danny, her mom calls after us.

When we're in the safety of her room, Beth pulls me close and whispers, Was that about last night?

Her scent is intoxicating, like I'm inhaling a drug that makes her room disappear and all I see is her face and the beautiful, worried expression on it. She grabs my hands and the drugs come in through the touch of her fingertips, emanating through my body.

No, I say. When my mom died, he was the first one there. Whenever he sees me, he's always trying to be nice to me, that's all.

She exhales relief and she smiles, and I want to hug her and kiss her. But I don't know how.

Now I'm not drunk and neither is she, and so we don't seem to know what to say. She sits on the corner of her bed and leans back on her elbows. Her hair falls back on her bedspread, and she asks if I want to sit down, so I do.

The walls of the room are covered in posters. There's an AC/DC poster of the *Highway to Hell* album cover, with the old lead singer, the one who died, and sneering Angus Young with his school uniform and devil horns and devil tail. Another poster with the lead singer of Poison with his shirt off and wearing makeup. Another of the Van Halen album cover with the little cherub with a cigarette in his hand. She has a vanity with scattered makeup tubes and hairspray bottles, and the mirror is pasted with photographs of friends. Some of them I recognize from school, some I've never seen before. There's even one of Craig, with Luke and Doug, leaning against the Nova. The whole room smells like Beth.

I wish I had a cigarette, Beth says.

Yeah?

I mean, I have one, but I just can't smoke in the house.

I look at her, not knowing what to say.

My mom doesn't know I smoke, she says. Well, I should say that she *pretends* she doesn't know. How come you don't smoke?

I just never started.

Don't, she says. It's a bad habit.

You could quit.

Yeah, but it just tastes so good.

If they taste so good, I say, how come they smell so bad?

She looks at me and I smile, and she smiles, and finally there's some levity in the room.

She asks if I want to listen to some music, and we spend several minutes looking at her cassettes, trying to decide what to play. They're piled in a shoebox, and she has a lot to choose from. More than me or Craig—but not more than us put together. We decide on Guns N' Roses' *Appetite for Destruction*. Skipping the obvious songs, we fast forward to the ones that are good but never get played anywhere.

We take turns picking songs to play for each other. We try to outdo each other, picking ones that aren't popular, even obscure, but still good. The songs that most people don't know but they should know. It's harder for me because these are her cassettes, and her taste is a little more popular than mine. There's no Iron Maiden. No Judas Priest. Only the newest Metallica, the one everyone's got. But we are having fun and this gives us something to talk about when we can't think of anything else. We play a lot of songs and talk about them, but then when she plays "Don't Know What You Got Till It's Gone" from Cinderella she gets quiet, and I know she's worried about what I'm thinking.

Sorry, she says.

It's okay, I say. It's a good song.

She smiles, but the mood has changed. Darkness is at the window. Sunset has come and gone, and night is here. Time has moved forward while we've been having fun, but now things are different. I look through her cassettes, trying to find one last song to listen to. I want to leave on a good song. But there's a knock on the door, and Beth's mom is standing there, telling us that it's time for me to get going so Beth can get ready for school tomorrow.

Come on, Mom, just a little more time, Beth says. My homework is done.

Danny, her mom says, do you need a ride home?

I tell her I don't, but she asks where I live and when I tell her she insists.

Beth asks to drive and her mom says no and Beth says, Why not? I have my permit.

They start arguing. I wish I could walk away, but I can only sit and listen as they argue, Beth saying that she's never going to learn if she's not allowed to drive and her mom saying that she needs more practice before she's ready to drive after dark.

I think of offering to call my brother to come get me, but Craig might not be home and I don't want my dad to do it.

The mom's boyfriend walks in and says that he will go and Beth can drive.

Fine, her mom says. You three go. Jesus Christ almighty.

Beth says, Just forget it.

This is not what Beth wanted. But it's too late.

Jared pulls his truck out of the driveway, moving it into the street—he says there's no way he's letting her drive it. Beth and I stand in the garage by her mom's Plymouth station wagon while we wait, and she shakes her head side to side and says, god, I hate him.

Beth in the driver's seat, Jared in the passenger seat, me in the back. Our breath comes out in smoky bursts in the blackness, and we ride in silence. The businesses in town are closed early because it's Sunday, and only a few cars drive around, as if a blizzard has hit and driven everyone indoors. But there is no snow, no storm, only the cold and a feeling that hangs over the land like sadness and suffering.

Craig's car is in the driveway. I'm relieved.

Thank you for the ride, I say.

Thanks for hanging out, Beth says, turning and looking at me in the backseat.

Jared sits, his head tilted back on the seat, as if he's sleeping.

I don't know what else to say so I say that I'll see Beth tomorrow in school.

She smiles and I smile, but her smile is forced and this good-bye isn't like the good-bye from earlier today, at sunrise, when we kissed, but I don't know what I can do about it so I step out of the car and walk up the steps and onto the front porch where no light is on to welcome me home.

Dad is sitting in his recliner and I notice right away that his eyes are bloodshot and the coffee table is scattered with beer cans. He usually drinks slowly all day on Sundays and doesn't get this drunk. I know that he's been in here, getting angrier and angrier, drinking one after another, waiting for me to get home. Down the hall, Craig is listening to AC/DC, the sad slow song off of *Who Made Who* that he listens to sometimes when he and Gretchen fight. The only song on the album sung by the dead singer—"Ride On" it's called—where he says over and over that he's lonely.

Where the hell have you been? Dad says.

Sorry, I say. I should have called.

My work clothes are in the goddamn washing machine.

I stare at him.

That's what you were worried about?

I can't work in wet clothes.

You could put your own clothes in the dryer.

Don't get lippy with me, boy.

Lippy?

Then he's up and out of his chair. One hand is gripping my jacket in an iron clamp and the other is pointing a finger in my face like the barrel of the Magnum. His breath is a furnace of beer and cigarettes and something else, something rotten and sour and sick.

I work hard to—

He stops because Craig is coming down the hall in long strides.

I told you he was at a girl's house, Craig says. Cut him some fucking slack.

Stay out of this, Dad shouts.

Leave him alone, Craig yells back.

Now they're facing each other, and I yell for them to stop. I'll do the laundry, I say.

But it's too late. A dam has busted. Dad turns away, kicks the coffee table, flipping it upside down and sending beer cans and ashes into the air.

Yeah, that's the answer, Craig shouts, and he closes his fist and punches a painting on the wall—a covered bridge in wintertime—and the glass breaks and the painting slides down the wall, hits the floor, and falls face forward onto the carpet. Let's just fucking break shit! Craig yells.

Your mother picked that out, Dad growls, and he lunges at Craig, but I catch him and throw him backward onto the couch and hold him there when he tries to struggle up. His face is red and his teeth are clenched like a rabid animal. I am crying and yelling for him to stop, please stop, and tears are coming down my face, and saliva is coming out of my mouth, and when Dad gives up I see in his face he can't believe that I could hold him.

He breathes in and out, in and out. My hand on his chest feels his heart pounding. I back away and look at Craig. His fists are clenched like hammerheads, and blood is dripping from the one he punched the picture with, drops of red that shine bright as they fall and then turn dark, almost black, when they hit the carpet.

Dad sits up, puts his head in his hands.

I'm sorry, boys.

His words are slurred.

It's just that, he continues, it's hard on me to support us on my own. Sometimes I wish your mother would have—

Don't say it! Craig shouts. He throws his hands up. How many times do we have to fucking hear it, Dad? *I wish your mother would have made it look like an accident so we could get the insurance money.* Jesus Christ!

He stomps away and I hear the front door open. He has no jacket on, just a tee shirt, but I hear his Nova start up, the rumbling of the engine, and tires spinning as he peels away from the house.

Dad sits and looks at the floor but I know he's looking at the past and the present and the future all at once, everything, his whole world through a lens of alcohol and sadness and rage. I go to put his work clothes in the dryer and get a washcloth and garbage can and vacuum to clean the glass and ash and blood out of the carpet.

Craig is gone and Dad is passed out, and I open my window and climb up the old TV antenna that doesn't work onto the roof. I do this in the summer usually, not the winter, and the metal triangle ladder is like ice on my hands. I lie on the shingles and look up at the sky and think. I shiver. The sky has cleared except for a few big white clouds, white rocky boulders floating without gravity in a sea of stars.

Water pools up in my eyes and leaks down from the corners. I'm not crying, at least I don't think I am, but the water is there anyway, so I sit up and I look around at the neighborhood. No sound. No movement. It's as if a plague wiped everyone out like in that Stephen King book I never finished. I know there's life inside the houses. But there's no movement. And the neighborhood is silent. In the distance, I hear the faint sound of cars on the highway and, even farther, the horn of a train. It's a quiet night if I can hear the train.

Somewhere, out there, Craig is cruising in the Nova. The engine rumbles; the tires squeal. He sits behind the windshield, scowling, his hand clenched on the steering wheel. The radio might be blasting or it might be silent. If he's really angry, he's forgotten to turn it on, and he's flying through the streets, passing cars, running stop signs.

I wish I was a ghost so I could float up and go look for him. Sometimes I think about Mom doing that. I picture her watching me right now, sitting next to me on the icy slab of the roof as I shiver in the cold. Sometimes I want her to be watching me. When I pray, if you could call it that, I pray to her. But I know there's no heaven and no hell, and there can't be ghosts or angels watching over us.

C raig shakes me awake in the morning.

Hurry up and get ready for school, he says. He's sitting on the edge of my bed, his arm on my shoulder. We'll go cruise for a bit.

The room is dark. The only light is coming in from the hallway.

Okay, I say.

Craig used to drive me to school when he first got the Nova, but then he started driving Gretchen and he didn't want to drive me anymore. That was when I was in middle school, and he would drop me off at the door. Everyone else either had to ride the bus or was being dropped off by their parents, but I got to be dropped off by my older brother, pulling up in a loud car. It was hard to go back to riding the bus, but I couldn't hold it against him. I knew he and Gretchen were making out.

He flips my light switch on his way out. I look for clothes to wear. I put on the jeans I wore yesterday and a long-underwear shirt, and then overtop that I put on a Grim Reaper tee shirt. The band sucks but the tee shirt is cool, and even though it says *rock you to hell* on the back, none of the teachers ever make me change.

I head to the bathroom to pee but Dad's in there on the toilet, and I can smell cigarettes and shit from outside the door. I start to make breakfast but Craig tells me to forget it, let's get something from McDonald's.

The car's already warming up, he says.

I notice it rumbling out front. And then our jackets are on and we're out the door in the cold and pulling away, in the opposite direction of school, the Nova speeding fast through the street. We head away from town, with fields on both sides, the fallow soil brown in all directions. The morning is just turning light, the air going from black to gray, and Craig speeds through low patches of fog. The street is wet with dew but Craig accelerates without a care.

The Nova's seatbelts are old, the kind where you have to pull the waist and shoulder belts separately. It's a pain in the ass so we never wear them.

Get a tape, Craig says. Something good.

I open the glove box and rummage through the cassettes.

Judas Priest? I say, holding the tape up.

Yeah!

It's a homemade cassette, one that Craig compiled one afternoon, laboring over all our Judas Priest albums—his and mine combined—to make his own personal greatest hits collection.

I slide the cassette into the stereo and we wait, neither of us remembering which song is first. The guitar starts and we both know it's "Heading Out to the Highway."

Dude, Craig says, slapping the steering wheel, this is perfect.

We're cruising down the back roads, away from town, as the world lights up. It's a gray morning, but the sun glows to the east, and the warmth is enough to cause steam to rise from the road, and we drive through it all, steam and mist and grayness and sadness. Craig turns up the volume. It's a perfect morning, listening to Rob Halford belt out lyrics and K.K. Downing and Glenn Tipton on the dual guitars. It's times like these that I can forget everything.

There's a digital clock on the stereo, but it's broken and just displays meaningless green vertical and horizontal lines. Craig has an old watch in the glove box, and normally I would look at it and worry and say we should be getting to school now. But I stop myself this time. I lean back and look out the window and watch the houses. They blur by, like we're traveling at supersonic speed.

But then Craig seems to know that we need to get to school because we're heading back into town. I'm disappointed, but the morning couldn't last forever.

He turns onto Mabry Street to go into town the back way, and he presses the gas pedal down and accelerates past a car even though another is coming in the other lane. He whips back over into our lane, and the Nova speeds faster and faster. My stomach lifts when we hit a dip in the road.

Up ahead, signs say REDUCE SPEED and SPEED LIMIT 35 because we're heading into a curve. Everyone calls this Dead Man's Curve, but I'm not sure if anyone has actually died here. Craig doesn't slow down. He hugs the inside of the curve and I grab my seat to keep from falling over.

Craig says, Thirty-five, my ass. I'm going—

The rear tires slide and screech and we start to go sideward, and Craig let's off the gas and turns into the skid. The car jerks and I'm thrown into the dashboard first and then back into the seat. We're in the other lane, and a car is coming, and the Nova fishtails as Craig tries to control it. The car up ahead honks and Craig yanks the wheel back into our lane, and then we're going forward, his foot back on the gas, leaving a cloud of rubber smoke and squiggly zigzag skid trails behind us.

Holy shit, bro! Craig says.

He smiles and I smile back, and he drives on, now going close to the speed limit but still over it.

I can't believe you pulled that out, I say.

Have faith, he says. I know how to drive this beast.

He leans over and pats the Nova on the dashboard like it's a pet.

I just need new tires, he says. These ones are as bald as a baby's ass.

We get closer to town and leave the fields and trees and then we're to the houses. The rich part of town, Monroe Village, is coming up.

There's that asshole Jamie Fergus's house. Craig points.

The house is bigger than I could imagine any family needing, two stories with big white columns on the front porch like a Southern mansion in the movies. Jamie's Camaro is nowhere to be seen.

Craig lifts his hand and gives the house the middle finger. Then we're past it and coming up on Main Street. The streets are crowded with cars: people going to work and kids going to school.

He pulls into the McDonald's drive-through and orders us both breakfast. While we're waiting on the food, he hands me a wad of folded bills and says, Here, if you're gonna have a girlfriend, you oughta have a few bucks to take her out.

There's a folded one dollar bill on the top, maybe five or six bills underneath.

Craig, you don't—

Just take it, Danny. I've got a little saved up from working. He thrusts with his hand, holding the money closer, and the woman appears at the window, holding a bag toward him.

Come on.

Thanks, I say, and I take the money.

I want to unfold the bills and look at them, but that might be rude, so I take the money and slide it into the inside pocket of my jacket.

No problem, he says, setting the bag of food on the seat between us and pulling away. Don't screw it up with that girl. If she makes you happy, make her happy.

Okay, I say, and I grin because he's never given me advice about girls.

As we're heading toward school, I know we're late because of the light of the sky and the traffic on the street. If we were on time, we would see more cars from the kids at school. But all of the cars are adults, no students.

You know, Danny, Craig says, keeping his eye on the road but tilting his head toward me. You're really the only thing in this world I care about.

Suddenly I feel shaky.

I guess I love Gretchen, he says, but that's different and that will fade. You're my brother and my best friend and I want you to know I'd do anything for you.

I squeeze my lips together, trying not to cry. I want to tell Craig that I feel the same way about him but if I open my mouth my voice will crack and it will be all over—I'll be sobbing.

He pulls into the parking lot at school and instead of finding a parking spot in the back, he pulls up toward the front door at the drop-off area and stops the car.

I'm gonna skip today, he says. We're late already so I might as well not go.

I swallow and say, I'll come with you. My voice cracks a little but I'm able to keep it together.

Nah, Craig says. You got a real chance at doing good in school. I don't want you to screw that up just to hang out with me for a day.

You got a chance too.

Shit, Craig says. We both know I ain't going to college.

But—

Danny, I'm skipping and you're staying. That's how it's going to be. I'm still your older brother.

Now I feel like crying again because I want to tell him that not only do I feel all the things he said about me, I feel even more. I feel the pressure of the world around me, pushing in on me, and the only thing holding it off from crushing me to nothing is Craig. We're in a dome or a bubble and if I was alone, the pressure would flatten me, but Craig's there and he doesn't even have to try and he holds off the weight. He just holds it up—the force of life and death and all that is—as if it's not even there.

I love you, Danny, Craig says.

He's never said this before, and I want to say it back but I can't open my mouth because I'll start to cry. He sees me holding my mouth tight, biting my lips, my chin quivering like a six-year-old who's just been spanked. So when I don't say it back he just smiles.

I open the door even though I don't want to and step out into the cold. I turn back as I'm walking and he lifts his arm to wave and I wave back. He waits till I'm inside the door. I stand there, just inside the first set of double doors, and watch as he drives away, the exhaust of the Nova like breath in the cold air. I lean my head against the cold glass and watch him disappear, and now the tears are coming down my cheeks and there's no stopping them.

His car is gone for a long time and yet I still stare out the window, my head against the door, feeling the tendrils of cold coming through the doorjamb. I stare at the soccer field and the playground at the elementary school and the ashen clouds floating through the sky. I don't even think about going to class until Mr. Segal, the shop teacher, comes up behind me and asks me what I'm doing.

Nothing, I say, wiping my eyes.

You okay? he asks.

Yeah, I say, turning toward him but not making eye contact.

You sure?

Uh-huh.

You running late today?

I nod.

He studies me for a moment then reaches into his pocket. He starts to fill out a green slip—an excused tardy—and says, Here, give this to your teacher.

You don't have to give me special treatment, I say.

He stops writing and puts the pad away.

Fine, he says.

I turn away, and he calls after me but I keep walking.

I go to the restroom and my locker and when I walk into my first class, I'm thirty minutes late. My English teacher says, Danny, where's your pass? I say I don't have one. She tells me I'm going to have to go to the principal's office.

The halls are empty. I feel strange, almost like I'm a ghost walking through an abandoned world. Like my spirit has stayed in the school and time has moved forward and the rest of the students have moved on, graduated, class after class. The school exists, but I'm always alone in it. And I suppose that's true, only it's not me who's always alone in it. It's me now but in a few years it will be someone else. There's people like me, I guess, in every school. Maybe not people whose moms killed themselves but people who feel just as alone.

In the office, there's a student worker, a freshman girl who is in some of my classes, and she says hi. We went to the same middle school and elementary—back when I wasn't quite the way I am now—and so I know her a little even though I haven't talked to her in a few years. She has braces and freckles and wears a purple sweater, and it's funny because when we were little kids we might not have been that different. But now she's a teacher's pet working in the office during study hall and I'm a hood with hair down my neck and a Grim Reaper tee shirt. But she's never been anything but friendly to me and I can't remember ever being mean to her.

I tell her I was late and I don't have an excuse.

She looks toward the offices down the hall. The principal and vice principal and whoever else has offices back there. She's thinking about how to give me a green pass. There's probably a way to do it and she probably would for a good friend. But a good friend of hers wouldn't be late and if she was she would have an excuse. But still the girl, Stephanie is her name, is thinking hard about it, and I don't want her to do it. It's not worth it to me.

Mr. Kerr walks out of his office. I don't know what his title is, but he is in charge of discipline. He wears a short-sleeve button-down shirt, even in winter, to show off his muscular arms. He must work out a lot, but there isn't any real strength in him, not like Dad or Sergeant Frederickson—I can tell just by looking.

What's going on? he says to me, speaking as if he knows me even though we have never spoken.

I'm late, I say. Mrs. Carver won't let me in class without a pass.

You got a note from your mom or dad?

I glance at Stephanie and see her discomfort. She opens her mouth to speak but stops herself.

I don't have a note.

Why are you late?

I just am.

No reason?

He's only a foot or so from me now, staring at me, testing me.

No reason.

You've gotta have a reason.

I don't.

He squints at me, looking up.

Well, he says, you missed almost the whole first period. That's an hour detention after school. How does that strike you?

How does that strike me?

Yeah.

I don't know what you mean.

How do you feel about that?

I don't care.

You don't have a reason for being late to school and you don't care about detention?

He frowns and shakes his head. He picks up the red notepad from the desk and pulls a pen out of his left breast pocket. I stand and wait.

He hands the slip to me and says that he's signing me up for detention and tells me where to go. I'm sure he doesn't know my name but he will ask Stephanie as soon as I leave.

I raise my hand to her as I turn to go, and she smiles and mouths the word sorry.

Hey, Mr. Kerr says as I'm opening the door to leave.

I turn.

You better start caring about things, he says. Life's going to be long and hard if you don't care about things.

I stare at him for a second, trying to think of some clever comeback. Instead I just turn away in silence. What I wanted to say was that he was wrong about me and about the world. I do care and that's what makes life so hard. Life would be easier if you didn't care, if you could walk through it numb, not feeling any emotions. I feel too much. And life is too hard for someone who feels too much.

In study hall, I ball my jacket into a pillow and lay my head on it. I'm asleep when the teacher nudges me.

Danny, she says. You have to go to the guidance counselor's office.

I rise and wipe drool from my mouth. I didn't realize I was so tired.

Mrs. McCreary hands me the slip. Everyone watches me because that's what everyone does—you always wonder if someone's in trouble. But this is common for me—Craig and I get these slips from the guidance counselor every few weeks. It's just to check on us after what happened with Mom. Craig taught me how to handle Mr. James, the guidance counselor. He said Mr. James would ask about personal feelings and our home life and stuff like that, but Craig said that if I asked him questions about college and careers and things like that, questions to keep him occupied, it would steer him away from the kinds of questions I didn't want to talk about. And it works. It makes him feel like he's being productive if he can talk to us about our future, keeps him distracted.

I stop in the restroom on my way and see lines on my face where I was sleeping, red indentations that look like scars, like maybe I was in a knife fight or was stabbed with the broken end of a beer bottle. I splash water on my face but the marks won't go away. I walk to the counselor's office anyway.

Mr. James smiles when I come in, and he beckons me to a seat. He is a short man—not fat just built thick in the middle—with thinning blond hair. He has a gentle voice and is easy for most of the kids in school to talk to. There's a big debate at school about whether he's a fag, but most of the kids really like him. I always thought it was wrong that so many people liked him but said they wouldn't if they found out for sure that he was gay.

Been taking a nap? he says with a sly grin. Not getting enough sleep at night?

Just last night.

Oh yeah. What were you doing last night?

He makes the questions sound harmless enough with the tone he uses, but I know he's looking for problems at home.

I got caught up in some movie on TV, I say.

Danny, he says. You've got to remember you have school in the morning. Remember your priorities.

I look around the office and study the posters. Picturesque landscapes with inspirational slogans and quotes from people throughout history. I read one with a quote from Eleanor Roosevelt:

The future belongs to those who believe in the beauty of their dreams.

Where's your brother today? Mr. James asks.

Sick.

Well, make sure your dad calls and lets us know. Right now we have him down as unexcused.

Now is when I should ask him about a career possibility, how to become a TV cameraman or a firefighter or some other diverting question. But I'm tired. Every time I come here is a performance, and the last few days have been tiring enough that I'm not sure I can pretend right now.

So how have you been, Danny?

I'm fine.

How are things at home?

They're fine.

Is there anything you'd like to talk about?

I lean forward and put my head in my hands and run my fingers through my hair and realize I'm not quite fully awake.

Well, I say, last night, I climbed up on my roof and was looking at the stars.

After the movie?

Yeah, after the movie. And I was thinking about how each star is a sun, right?

Yes, he says. Some are actually a lot bigger than our sun. Some thousands of times the size of our sun.

I look at him, surprised.

He goes on. There are some stars, he says, that if they were in our solar system, they would take up the space from the sun all the way out to Jupiter.

That doesn't seem possible, I say.

I picture those models of the solar system I'm always seeing in school. Mom helped me make one once. It wasn't to scale, but Jupiter, the biggest planet, was way out in space.

Well, he says, if you want more information about all that, you'll have to ask one of your science teachers. But go on. I'm interested.

It's nothing.

Please, Danny. You were sitting on the roof.

I look at Mr. James. I don't feel right this morning, something is different about the world or about me, so I decide to just tell him.

I was thinking about the stars and how many there were, I say, and it made me think about the planet and how many people there were. Kind of like, maybe there's a star for everyone, you know. Maybe we can't see them all in the sky, some are so far away even our biggest telescopes haven't spotted them yet. Maybe there's a star for every person.

Maybe, Mr. James says, nodding.

I know it doesn't work that way. Not really. But it got me to thinking about how each person is a world, you know. Not a planet, but a *world*. A universe. An existence.

Now he looks at me quizzically, like he's not following.

This world doesn't exist without me, I say. If I died right now, the world would end. It's gone.

He opens his mouth to speak but stops.

I know the world goes on, I say. I know the other kids at school, their worlds go on, but my world is over. It's blackness. It's not even blackness. It's nothing. An apocalypse has just happened. The sun has just blinked out. The world—a whole universe—just ceased to exist.

Danny, I'm not sure I'm following you.

When someone dies, I tell him, the world ends. That's what I'm trying to say. A whole universe is extinguished. Every time someone dies, it's like the sun going out. Just like that—I snap my finger—and all that is and all that ever was and ever will be is gone.

Mr. James gulps. He's never heard me talk like this.

Danny, when someone dies, it's very sad, but the world doesn't end.

You're wrong, I say. That's exactly what happens.

Danny, he says, do you—

Wait, I say. Let me just think about how to explain this.

We sit in silence for a few seconds, and he opens his mouth to speak again and I cut him off even though I'm not ready to talk again.

If I died tomorrow, I know that everyone else would go on living. I know that my brother and my dad and you would still wake up in the morning and live your lives.

Danny—

But those are different worlds. You all live in different worlds. I live in my own world and when I die, that world is over. Armageddon. Apocalypse. Whatever you call it. No survivors. The sun—the source of all life in that world—has just been blown out like a birthday candle.

Mr. James is quiet.

And I just think that's sad, I say. It's just sad to think about how many times the world ends each day all over the world.

Danny, Mr. James says patiently, you're not making a lot of sense. But I want to talk about this feeling of sadness you mentioned.

Just forget it, I say. It was just some stupid thought I had.

I want to help.

I look away from him, at the posters on the walls, then down at my feet.

Danny, are you sad?

I sit back.

I stare at him. I don't want to talk about this, I say.

Because if you're sad—

Of course, I'm sad, I snap. What the hell do you think?

He freezes.

I stand.

No wait, he says. Don't go yet.

I said I don't want to talk about it.

I reach for the door handle.

Wait, Danny, I—

I walk into the hallway, and after only a few steps, the bell rings and I'm suddenly surrounded by students. Dozens of other worlds around me, bumping up against mine, existing in the same space, the same realm, but all different universes. Different suns lighting different worlds, all waiting to be extinguished.

In math class, Beth comes and sits behind me just as the bell rings.

Hi, she whispers, smiling big.

I turn in my chair, and we start talking. The teacher, Mrs. Cox, begins to talk about theorems but Beth and I continue to whisper, her leaning forward in the chair and me leaning back, my head turned enough that I can feel her breath on my cheek and smell her hairspray.

I think the whole school has heard about what happened, she whispers.

Really?

Yeah, she says. Trisha Barnhart asked me about it first thing this morning.

I look around and suddenly feel like everyone in the room is watching us. No one turns and looks, but I feel them *aware* of us. It's been a long time since I've felt noticed.

And then, Beth says, in second period—

Beth! Mrs. Cox says. Danny!

We face forward.

Do I need to separate you two?

We shake our heads.

Her eyes linger on me.

When she turns away, Beth leans back and is quiet. I hear her writing on a piece of notebook paper, then folding it, and I feel her hand on my shoulder. I grab the note as Mrs. Cox writes an equation on the board, talking about X and Y. No one has ever passed me a note before.

The note says,

I hear Jamie Fergus vows to get back at Craig

I stare at the words.

I can feel Beth waiting for me to write a response and pass it back, but I don't know what to say.

She starts a new note and passes it to me.

He's such a dick. I hope Craig kicks his ass again.

I turn my head to the side and nod so Beth can see me. I fold her notes and put them in my algebra book, deep into the back of the book in the chapters we won't get to this year.

At lunchtime, I walk into the cafeteria and get into line like always. People around me seem different than usual. I am always there without anyone noticing, taking up space but invisible otherwise. Now I feel the others looking at me. I see no glances, hear no whispers. But the air is different, like the atmospheric pressure has changed, and the cause of this change is me.

I look around for Beth.

Dawn from Saturday night, the one with the buttons on her jacket, walks up smiling.

Hey, Craig's Brother, she says, cutting into line with me. She says it just like that's my name: Craig's Brother.

How's it going? she asks.

Okay.

Crazy weekend, huh?

She looks around, wanting, as I do, for someone else to join us because neither of us knows what to say.

I look at her jacket. One of the buttons says,

If you love someone, set them free.
If they don't come back, hunt them down and kill them.

So where's Craig today? she asks. He wasn't in Government class.

I'm not sure, I say.

He wouldn't care if I told her he was ditching school, but still I don't tell her.

He's not sick, is he?

I frown and shrug my shoulders.

Another button on her jacket says,

That shirt is very becoming on you.
If I were on you, I'd be coming too.

He's going to get suspended if he keeps ditching, she says.

She has dark brown hair, like the pelt of an animal, and she could be pretty if she didn't wear so much black eye shadow.

You don't say much, do you, kid?

I look at her.

Nope.

She stares at me and then bursts out laughing.

Jesus, kid.

I smile too, and then I start laughing along with her, a good, hearty laugh that sounds strange coming from me.

Beth sidles up next to me from out of the throng of students.

What's so funny?

Dawn shakes her head, still smiling. Your boyfriend, she says. He's hilarious.

My insides churn at her use of the word boyfriend. I feel blood rushing to my head and hope my face isn't turning red.

Beth smiles and says, Oh yeah?

I shrug, and for whatever reason this makes Dawn start giggling again.

The lunch line moves forward, and as we step forward with it, Beth takes my hand and holds it in hers like maybe we are boyfriend and girlfriend.

At lunch, I'm eating my pizza square and laughing as Luke and another kid, a senior named Kenny, a chubby kid with a black tee shirt with a yellow Batman symbol on it, dare each other to eat gross concoctions they make with their food. I've been around them before, but I've never hung out with them or eaten lunch with them. I'm here with Beth and Dawn, and everyone acts as if I belong.

Luke squirts ketchup into his milk box, dumps green Jell-O in with it, and swirls it all up with his plastic spork. Kenny offers him five dollars to drink the whole thing. Luke does it, chugging it down like a beer. He grimaces, belches, and says it wasn't bad.

You are so gross, Beth says.

I'm laughing. I usually eat alone. The cafeteria is too crowded to actually get a table to yourself, so I typically find a table with empty seats and sit down, usually with other outcast freshmen, even though I'm not friends with them. We all sit together by default because we have nowhere else to sit. Today it's nice to sit somewhere else.

Kenny tries to win his money back by mashing up his green beans, pouring Hawaiian Punch into them, pouring someone else's milk in, hacking his own snotty saliva into the mess, mixing it all up, and then eating it. It takes him nine spoonfuls and Luke insists that he slurp up the liquid remnants with a straw. Kenny holds out his hand and Luke reluctantly gives the money back.

I'm going to be sick, Dawn says.

I know, Beth says, looking at me and rolling her eyes.

I'll give you all the money I have, Luke says to Kenny, if you make another batch of grossness like that but *I* spit in it this time.

Well, how much money do you have on you?

I'm not telling.

Well, that's dumb.

It's a gamble, Luke says, pushing his glasses up the bridge of his nose. I might have one dollar. I might have one hundred.

They argue this way for several seconds, and this makes me think about the money Craig gave me. It's in my jacket in my locker. I never looked at how much was there.

This is what I'm thinking about when Jamie Fergus walks up to our table.

He approaches flanked by two other jocks. One is Benji Johnson, a heavy kid everyone calls Moose because he's so big and can grow a full beard. He's the only person from the football team to make the all-state team besides Jamie. The other is someone I've seen around but don't know his name. He is smaller than me but has a certain wiry look to him, like he's probably quick. Fergus is wearing a sweater that's too tight for his muscles, and his cheek is swollen and the skin around his eye is purple and blue and yellowish on the edges.

Hey, Jamie, Kenny says, what happened to your face?

Dawn nudges him in the arm because of course he knows what happened.

Jamie ignores the question and stands beside me. He leans over, putting one fist down on the table next to my lunch tray and the other hand on the back of my chair. His face is close to mine and I smell his cologne.

I don't move or lean away.

Where's your pussy brother today?

I don't say anything. I stare forward, not making eye contact with anyone at the table. Jamie's fist sits on the table like the head of a sledgehammer.

I said where's your brother?

Jamie, Dawn says, why don't you leave the kid—

He grabs the back of my hair and tries to shove my head forward toward my plate, but I stand up and push him, and then we're standing face to face. Everyone at the table is up. Beth and Dawn are trying to get between us but the two other guys are holding them back.

Luke says, Hey, just leave him alone.

I can't see anything else because I'm staring Jamie Fergus in the eyes, but I sense that everyone in the cafeteria has turned and is looking at us.

The other night, Jamie looked Craig's height and I always think of Craig as being a good two inches taller than me, but now that we're face to face, Jamie Fergus can't be more than half an inch taller than me. He's bigger, broader, but knowing that I'm almost as tall means something to me, and I stand and I stare and I'm not afraid.

Touch me again, he says, and I will beat your ass.

I don't say anything. I just stare at him. Neither of us has blinked yet, but now he does.

One of Jamie's friends mutters, Here comes Mr. Kerr.

Jamie turns and looks but still I'm staring at him. He looks back at me, takes a deep breath and steps back, and says, I didn't come here to fight you, kid. Just tell your dickhead brother—

I'm not your messenger.

His patience snaps and he gets in my face again. Tell your brother I'm gonna make him cry worse than he did when your momma killed herself.

He leans back as if that's the final word on subject. I spit in his face.

There's a split second pause and I know what's going to happen. Then it happens. His fist comes up fast. I turn but still take the brunt of the blow in the face. It knocks me back and I trip over my chair and go down on my back. He probably thinks *that* will be the final word on the subject, but I'm up fast and try to tackle him. He grabs hold of me, spins me around. Both my feet leave the ground. One foot hits someone as I'm flying, and then I'm on the ground again, on my knees this time, my arms still tangled up with his. I can't believe how strong he is. I rise to my feet, and I try to get an arm free to hit him, but other arms are pulling us away. Jamie lets go but I keep struggling for a few seconds before I realize the arms belong to Mr. Kerr and Mr. Delaney.

I'm breathing heavy. My shirts are pulled up and halfway off.

Just settle down, Mr. Delaney says.

He's a math teacher, and he's fat and out of shape. His face looks red from the strain. He stands in front of me and Mr. Kerr stands in front of Jamie.

I straighten my shirts. My Grim Reaper tee shirt is stretched out, the neck hole twice its former size. The elastic sleeve of my long undershirt is stretched out too, hanging loosely around my wrist.

Jamie's face looks just as red as Mr. Delaney's. His muscles bulge through the sweater and now, after everything is over, he finally looks scary. There is no way I could have beaten him. His broad chest rises and falls. He stares at me, exhaling deep breaths through his nose like a bull. Spittle is still on his face, droplets here and there and a big glob clinging to his brow above the blackened eye.

Hey, Jamie, Kenny calls to him, you've got a little something on your face.

Several people start laughing. He clenches his jaw and wipes the spit away with his hands.

I'm going to kill you, you little—

Come on, Mr. Kerr says. Let's all go to the office.

Jamie turns and the crowd parts, and the rest of us follow. Beth watches as we walk by, her eyes moist.

She mouths the words, I'm sorry.

I shrug. I don't know what else to do. I feel like I should apologize to her.

We are escorted into the office and told to sit in chairs at each end of a row of four. Two chairs separate us. I sit and face forward at a row of offices: Mr. Kerr's, Principal Bell's, the assistant principal, whatever her name is. Mr. Delaney stands with us while Mr. Kerr goes to find the principal.

You boys just stay there and cool down, he says and wanders off.

He doesn't go far enough that he can't see us, but far enough for Jamie to mutter to me, You're fucking dead. You and your brother both.

I turn and he's staring at me. The redness in his face is gone. He seems relaxed almost, except for his eyes.

I'm gonna bash your head in.

I want to say something back, something tough, but I can't think of what to say. Mr. Delaney returns, telling us to sit tight because Mr. Kerr will be back soon with Principal Bell. He is standing and we are sitting, and there is silence, and in the background we can hear the secretaries talking about *Dallas*.

What happened to your eye, Jamie? Mr. Delaney asks. Was this payback for something that happened over the weekend?

Jamie laughs. No, I was playing basketball down at the church and caught an elbow when I was going in for a layup. Made the shot though.

Mr. Delaney chuckles. His belly bounces.

I lean my head back against the wall and close my eyes. Mr. Kerr arrives with Mr. Bell, and they direct Jamie and me into the office.

We have to sit next to each other. Mr. Bell sits behind his desk and Mr. Kerr leans against the wall behind Bell, with his arms crossed. Mr. Bell has tired eyes and everyone makes fun of his toupee, but this is the first time I've been close to him and I can't really tell the difference. It looks like hair to me.

He takes a deep breath to show how disappointed he is in us and then says, Well, Mr. Kerr has told me what happened, but why don't you boys tell me your version.

It's just a big misunderstanding, Jamie says, leaning forward and speaking in what my dad would call a bullshit politician tone. You see, he says, Danny's brother owes me twenty bucks and was supposed to give it to Danny to pass along to me. But I guess he forgot. When I asked him for it today, he thought I was trying to steal his lunch money.

He smiles, and I can tell Bell and Kerr know he is lying but that they are relieved to hear a story they can pretend to believe.

It's my fault, Jamie says. I should have communicated better. I admire the kid for standing up to me to tell you the truth.

Mr. Kerr and Mr. Bell actually nod their heads in agreement.

Mr. Bell says, Jamie, you've got to use your head better than this. When you go to the university, they'll take your scholarship away for something like this.

I know. This was a good lesson for me to learn while I'm still in high school.

Mr. Bell turns to me.

Danny, that's your name, right?

I nod.

Do you agree that's what happened in the lunchroom?

No.

He scowls. He turns to look at Mr. Kerr, and Mr. Kerr shrugs his shoulders. Bell looks back at me.

That isn't what happened in the cafeteria?

I shake my head.

Would you care to tell us what happened?

No.

What?

I said no.

And why not?

It's not your concern.

I'm the principal of this school. Everything that happens here is my concern.

I say nothing.

I'm not going to ask again. I want to know your side of what happened.

No.

He sits back in his seat in frustration.

You want us to call your father?

I look in his eyes. Go ahead.

He drops his eyes. Mr. Kerr didn't know who I was earlier, but now they both do, and they know that calling my dad would do no good just like it doesn't when they call him about Craig.

Quiet. Everyone stares. I look at no one. I stare at a picture on Mr. Bell's desk. It shows him and his wife and two little girls, probably about ten and eight, smiling in front of a fake backdrop of flowers. The girls are happy, purely innocent and unaware of the world and the horrors it holds. Mrs. Bell smiles but her eyes divulge a hidden sadness.

Mr. Bell takes a deep breath and opens his mouth to speak but then stops.

Mr. Kerr says, Danny already has detention today for coming late to school. I think he's having a bad day, and that's why he's being contrary.

Jamie's explanation sounds reasonable in light of Danny's unwillingness to cooperate.

Mr. Bell nods his head, and Jamie and I sit and wait.

Mr. Kerr continues. We could give Danny detention for not cooperating, but since he already has it—and since he probably got the worst of it in their little spat—maybe we should just let these two off with a warning.

Mr. Bell warns us that normally fighting would warrant a suspension, and I know that the only reason we aren't suspended is because they don't want to suspend Jamie Fergus because of who he is and they don't want to suspend me because they know I didn't start it.

They ask Jamie to stay for a few minutes to talk about something "unrelated," and they tell me I'm free to go. As I rise, Mr. Bell asks if I'm okay.

Looks like you're going to have a bruise, he says. Are you hurt?

He could never hurt me, I say.

Boy, Mr. Kerr says, there's no reason to try to act all tough.

I'm not tough, I say, and I'm the only one in this room who hasn't been acting since we got here.

I turn and leave and after I close the door behind me, I pause in the hallway and I hear them all laughing at me, Jamie laughing with them like they're all part of the same club.

I stop in the restroom across from the office and look at myself in the mirror. My cheek is swollen and red, starting to turn purple, but it's nowhere near as bad as Jamie's eye from when Craig hit him. My Grim Reaper shirt is ruined, and I take it off and wad it into a ball and hold it in my fist. I stare at myself, and I imagine fighting Jamie again, doing things differently, having more time, knocking him out, hurting him badly, winning this time.

I leave and walk down the hall, away from the cafeteria and toward my locker. The halls are empty, with everyone eating or in class. The clock says the bell will ring in two minutes, and then people will be everywhere.

I think about the fight, and I think about a fight to come. What will happen next. What I can do.

I think about sneaking into his house at night and holding the Magnum against his head. I push those thoughts away and just think about fighting him. But then the thoughts are back and the gun is in my hand and I know not to squeeze the trigger because I understand the finality of what that means, but I'm just in my head so I do it anyway.

Beth finds me in the hall before my last period and asks what happened. I tell her we got off with a warning.

She looks at my eye and winces and makes a noise with her teeth, like a hissing cat. Ouch, she says. Does it hurt?

It's okay. Just throbs a little.

She reaches to touch the bruise and stops her hand and tucks my hair back behind my ear instead.

I'm so sorry.

My shirt's ruined, I say, pulling it out of the locker and holding it up for her to see, front and back.

That sucks. That was a badass shirt.

People walk by in the hall, and again I feel like everyone is looking at me.

You want a ride after school? Beth asks. Some of us are going to hang out. You want to come along.

I have detention.

I thought you just got a warning.

This is for something else. I smile at her. I'm having a bad day, I say.

She tells me that they'll come back for me.

The hall is clearing out, and that means the bell is about to ring. Beth stands on her tiptoes and kisses me gently on the cheek, right where I was hit, and it's over before I know it and she's walking down the hall away from me, but I can still feel waves of her kiss emanating through me.

The last period of the day, I sit by the window in the back row and look out toward the parking lot. The seniors get out an hour earlier than the rest of the students, and they walk through the parking lot, heading to their cars. The sun is out, but the air looks cold. People walk with their heads down and their hands stuffed into coats.

Jamie Fergus is walking with Gretchen. They are on the sidewalk leading toward the parking lot. They're holding hands, with Gretchen's other hand buried in her leather jacket and Jamie's other hand tucked into his jeans. She is looking up at him, her yellow hair bouncing around her purple scarf, the one Craig bought her. She looks at him the way she once looked at Craig, like she is a deer and he is a headlight and the rumbling engine from a car bearing down on her isn't enough to make her look away.

Behind them, Luke and Doug and Kenny walk toward the cars, and I know what's going to happen before it does.

Jamie Fergus turns his head as if he's sensed them. Like he's a predator and the wind has blown the scent of prey his way. He stops. He stares. Gretchen keeps walking and talking. She comes to the end of his arm and is pulled back like a dog on a chain.

Luke, Doug, and Kenny don't see him.

The glass on the windows is beginning to fog. I slide my desk over and reach out my arm and wipe the window. Mr. Staub is lecturing about the five rivers of Hades in Greek mythology.

Outside, Fergus is calling to Kenny and the others. I can't hear the words, but it's like a silent movie: I don't need to. He is talking to Kenny, his face red with anger. He is asking Kenny why he doesn't make a smartass remark now. Jamie is threatening him, leaning over him, telling him, Come on! Come on!

Kenny is shaking his head, laughing uncomfortably. He is saying that he won't fight Jamie. He is a fat kid with a big mouth, and he knows Jamie will win.

This just infuriates Jamie more. Someone shouldn't talk shit and not be willing to back it up. He wants Kenny to beg for mercy or to fight, but Kenny does neither. He says something like, Does it make you feel tough to pick on the fat kid?

Jamie takes a step closer and might do something—shove him or hit him—but Gretchen pulls at his jacket, telling him to stop. She's telling him that he will be suspended if he gets caught fighting. I wipe the window.

Mr. Staub is talking about the River Styx, which serves as the border between Earth and the Underworld, and is guarded by the boatman Charon. The Greeks put coins in the mouths of the dead so they could pay Charon for passage.

Jamie raises his arms, indicating to Gretchen that he won't do anything stupid, and he begins to turn away.

Kenny looks relieved, and he and Luke and Doug walk away.

Jamie turns, fast as a snake, and he's on Kenny, one hand on his shoulder and the other drawn back in a fist. He punches Kenny—one, two, three times—right in the lower back. In the kidneys.

Kenny screams—I can't hear it but I can see it—and reaches backward as he falls forward. He hits the sidewalk on his stomach, hitting his chin against the pavement.

Jamie and Gretchen are walking away, Jamie a step ahead of her, his hands in his pockets, his head looking around, swiveling on his shoulders like a hawk.

Kenny stays down, lying like a stabbing victim. Doug and Luke crouch over him. Luke yells at Jamie, but Jamie ignores him.

No one in the class is aware of what happened outside.

Kenny sits up, his belly fat hanging out from his shirt and jacket, and even from this distance I can tell that he is crying. Luke and Doug help him stand, and he walks tentatively, as if each step hurts.

Mr. Staub says that the River Lethe is the river of oblivion, and anyone who drank from its water would lose all memory of his earthly life.

After detention, I open my locker and reach for my jean jacket and I remember the money. Down the hall, a janitor is vacuuming. Otherwise, no one is around. School is over and the place is empty. I reach into the pocket and pull out the wad of bills. Below the one dollar on top, I fold back a twenty, and then another and another and then lose count. I have to straighten them and count them out to myself like a bank teller. Twenty. Forty. Sixty. Eighty. One hundred. Twenty. Forty. Sixty. Eighty. One hundred.

I stare at the money: two hundred and one dollars.

I thought maybe he'd given me twenty. Fifty if I was lucky.

I look around as if someone might be watching, and I put the money back in my jacket.

I stand outside in the cold, waiting. A few students—a couple I saw from detention, one or two others staying late for some other reason—walk to the parking lot. With the rest of the cars gone, their vehicles look abandoned out among the empty white lines.

The air is crisp and I ask myself how long I will wait. The busses are gone, so I'll have to walk if Beth and her friends don't come.

The breeze blows me, pushes my hair back from my face. Sometimes I like the cold. When you inhale it into your lungs, there's something about it that makes you feel sharp and awake. If you're in it too long it numbs you, but when you first step into it, the cold wakes you. Makes you feel alive. I don't feel alive enough.

I sit down on the curb, the sidewalk cold through my jeans. I rest my arms on my knees and look out at the empty field behind the school. The dirt is gray and frozen. The sky above is blue. I lie back on the pavement and look upward. A few clouds—white and wispy—float overhead. I try to see objects in them, but I can't. They're just clouds.

What I think about sometimes is this: a gun pressing up against my skin—my cheek, my forehead, my temple. Sometimes it's the Magnum and sometimes it's Dad's shotgun or his little .38 Special or another gun. Mostly it's the Magnum because that's what Mom used. And I imagine the feeling of the gun. I imagine this when I'm in my room at night, listening to music. When I'm in class. When I'm hurting real bad inside, and even when everything is okay, I think about a gun pressing against my head and I think about the trigger being pulled. Sometimes I pull the trigger and sometimes it's someone else. It doesn't matter who. What matters is the gun—this simple metal machine—is pressed against my head and the trigger moves. It strains against its springs, just slightly, just enough, a squeeze, and the gun goes off.

Sometimes I think of the bullet going through my head in slow motion. Most people think of bullet holes as entrance and exit holes but they don't really think of the tunnels that bullets dig. The connection between the entrance and exit is too abstract somehow, and they think the bullet has teleported from one explosion to the other. But the hole goes clear through, just as if you've been stabbed with a thin sword, a rapier like the one that killed Romeo's best friend in the play we read in English class. And so I picture the tunnel being dug in slow motion, but it's not being dug through solid earth, it's being dug through skin and bone and brain, and once the hole is punched through, the tunnel collapses like a muddy mine shaft falling in behind the bullet-shaped drilling machine.

But other times I try to picture it all—the bullet through the head—in real time, as fast as it would happen. As fast as you could snap your fingers. Faster. The hole isn't dug from one end to the other—it appears, like a bolt of lightning, all at once. Your skull is broken in where the bullet entered and blasted out where it exited, and there is blood and brain splattered everywhere, and your body is jerking, just a few final spasms. And I'm picturing this happening to me. But the reality is this: when you kill yourself, you wouldn't feel any of it. Unless you mess it up, the bullet will go through so fast you won't hear the shot, you won't feel the bullet enter your skull. You won't even feel the gun kick in your hand. You'll start to squeeze the trigger, just start to squeeze it. And then the lights will go out. Not even that. Because there isn't even blackness on the other side. People say blackness is the absence of color, but what happens when there's the absence even of blackness?

I heard that if you're born blind, you never know what blackness is. If you can see when you're born and you go blind, then that's what you see: blackness. But if you're born blind, your mind never comprehends color, not even black. Maybe when you die, it's like that—there's no color to comprehend. The same with the rest of the senses. It's like being born without understanding what sound is, what taste is, what sight is, and the rest. It's hard to imagine what it would be like to have none of those, but not only that: to have no *understanding* of what those are. That's what nothingness must be like.

But I think even this must be wrong—it assumes there's a *you* who can't sense these things. That's why people believe the soul goes on. It's too hard to grasp the idea of nothingness, of life stopping. Even if when you try to imagine what it's like to not exist, you find yourself thinking of something—some vague invisible consciousness in a sea of darkness—that goes on.

But I know the truth: there's no soul.

After Mom died, Dad said she was in heaven. He said he didn't give a shit what the Bible said about suicides: she was in heaven, goddamn it. When the police shrink asked me, I said heaven just seemed like a story made up to make us feel better. People want to picture an afterlife in heaven. Or they want to think of a person as just sleeping and not waking up—because sleeping is peaceful. People want to imagine a soul going on somehow, doing something. But that's all just mythology, like Thor and his magic hammer or Atlas holding up the earth. It's just make-believe. When you see your mother's brains like I have, you know there is no heaven, no hell, no soul. The person is not sleeping. The person is not in heaven or hell. The person is gone. Where life existed, now it does not. And to pretend life goes somewhere else is just a fantasy we invent because the fantasy makes it easier to mourn.

When a person dies, it's more like a story that's over. You can pretend the characters go on. You can imagine that they still exist. But it's over. There's nothing else there. Life happened. It stopped happening. The end.

I hear a car, and I sit up. Dawn's Toyota Corolla is pulling in and behind it is a Ford Taurus loaded with Luke, Doug, and Kenny. Beth is in the Toyota with Dawn and another girl in the back. I think her name is Gina. The Toyota pulls up next to me, and Beth rolls the window down.

Hey.

I rise up off the pavement.

We're going to the junkyard, she says. You wanna come?

Okay.

You'll have to get in with the boys. Gina's got her stupid tuba back there.

There's a big case sitting in the backseat.

Gina says, It's a baritone, assmunch.

That's okay, I say. Can we go by my house first? Maybe Craig's there.

Beth turns to Dawn, who is trying to light a cigarette but can't get a flame from her lighter.

No way, Dawn says, taking the cigarette out of her mouth. The junkyard is only for people who go to school.

Then she winks and says of course.

I walk to the other car.

What's up, Danny? Luke says.

The car smells of pot and their eyes are red.

We're going to my house first, I say. To see if Craig is home.

Great idea, Doug says.

He puts the car in drive and tears off after Dawn. When we get out on the two-lane, he tries to pass her, and they begin racing.

This is the most pathetic race in history, Luke says. Both these cars suck. Go to hell.

A car is coming and Doug hits the brakes and pulls behind Dawn, who holds up her middle finger so we can see it through the back window.

Everyone is laughing. Luke pulls out a pipe and packs it and lights it. He offers it to me, but I decline. Kenny says he's had enough. Doug grabs it and steers the car with his knee as he takes a hit. He passes it back. The air stinks sweetly from the smoke.

Luke and Doug are probably Craig's best friends. He used to hang out with them a lot before he started dating Gretchen. Luke wears glasses and takes the college-prep English and science classes. He's not real big or real tough, but he seems smart. Not just book smart, sort of wise and thoughtful. It seemed like everyone was always asking him for advice. Craig used to, but at some point he stopped.

Everyone's always teasing Doug about how stupid he is, but he's the one Craig was always calling when he needed help working on the Nova or to build a shelf or something like that. He's good at all the shop-class stuff. Kenny was never around that much—I'm not sure how much Craig likes him—but whenever I saw him he was always cracking jokes.

Kenny was laughing with everyone earlier but now he's somber. I tell him that I saw what happened out the window.

I'm sorry, I say. It's kind of my fault.

No. It's just that Jamie Fergus is a real dickhead.

That guy is an asshole, Luke says.

Doug says, You missed it, Kenny. When Craig laid him out Saturday night. He looked like a little baby.

Kenny says, I hope Craig kicks his ass again.

I sit quietly.

You think Craig can do it? Luke says. I mean, without having a roll of quarters in his hand?

No way, Doug says. Not in a fair fight. Not with Jamie Fergus.

I don't know, Luke says. I saw him fight that guy in Dell that time.

I know this story, but only a bare-bones version: Craig got in a fight; he won.

What happened? I ask.

Luke turns in the passenger seat so he can see all of us.

This stupid kid started some shit and got his ass kicked, that's what happened. I guess the guy thought Craig was checking out his girlfriend or something, which was bullshit. She was real white trash. Skinny as a corpse. Craig was looking at the dude's car, which was a badass Chevelle. We couldn't even see in the windows 'cause of the way the light was. The glass was just black, and Craig's looking at the car, just checking it out as we walked by.

Where was this? Kenny asks.

Doug turns the corner onto my road.

Taco Bell parking lot. The Taco Bell in Dell, not here.

I could go for some Taco Bell right now, Doug says.

Shut the hell up. I'm telling a story.

Just saying.

Anyway, Luke continues. The dude gets out of his car, starts saying, *Hey, you looking at my girl?*

Doug approaches my house. Craig's Nova isn't there. Dawn pulls in the driveway ahead of us, and Doug pulls in next to her. She rolls the window down, and I do too. The air is crisp.

Looks like he ain't home.

Nope.

You want to go inside? Leave a note or something?

Nah, I say.

Let's go to the junkyard, Luke says.

Let's go to Taco Bell first, Doug says.

Jesus Christ, Luke says, shaking his head.

Doug pulls out into the street, and Dawn follows.

Finish the story, Kenny says.

Oh yeah, Luke says, turning. Well, the guy starts yelling at Craig. They get in each other's faces, and a small crowd starts to gather around—it's Saturday night, you know?—and the guy says we need to go somewhere else if we're gonna fight, and Craig's like, *Fuck that, I'm going to get a burrito.* He turns to walk away and the guy grabs his arm and kind of turns Craig back and hits him in the face. Not a full-on blow. Craig turned in time, I think. Kinda like you turned a little today with Jamie Fergus, Danny.

Kenny looks at my face. Yeah, he says, you don't got much of a shiner, do you?

How big was the guy? I ask.

He was strong. Not Jamie Fergus strong, but he was muscular. I forgot to mention when they were arguing, the guy took his shirt off—it was the stupidest thing I'd ever seen—he just pulled his shirt off to show his muscles. He was one of those people you can see his stomach muscles. Kinda ripped like Jean-Claude Van Damme, but skinnier. I guess he was trying to intimidate your brother.

Well, Luke goes on, they just started hitting each other, and it was so fast. Not like a movie. Not like a boxing match either. Just a big blur of arms. I couldn't even tell you who landed how many punches—they were just whaling on each other. And then they were down on the ground. Wrestling around down there. I think the other guy did that, tried to get Craig down because he wasn't doing so good. But that was stupid because he didn't have a shirt on, and Craig got the guy on his back and was shoving him across the pavement, sort of pushing him like he was doing mountain climbers, and finally the guy starts yelling, *Stop, stop, stop.*

Craig kneels over him with his fist raised and the guy's hands are up in surrender. I thought he was going to keep hitting him, just pound him into unconsciousness, and Craig just says, kind of out of breath, *I wasn't looking at your girlfriend. She's a skank. I wouldn't fuck her with your dick.*

Kenny starts laughing and claps his hands.

Luke says, The fucked up thing is that both of them were covered in blood. I mean covered. It was all over Craig. But Craig didn't have a scratch on him. We went to a gas station and he went inside and cleaned up. He didn't have a mark on him. Not a bruise. The blood was all the other guy's.

Jesus, Kenny says.

The other guy was messed up, Luke says, I'm telling you. I turned and looked as we were leaving. His friends were helping him, and his back was all ripped up from the pavement. It was shredded. It looked like someone had taken a cheese grater to it.

After Doug gets his Taco Bell, our two cars head off to the junkyard. It's the first really sunny day in weeks. Around us, the town is busy with other people from school driving around. Usually, I'm home by now, having ridden the bus and missed all the after-school bustle. It's strange to think how one weekend seems to have changed things. Now maybe I have friends.

What about Jamie Fergus? I say. Have you ever seen him fight?

Kenny and Doug and Luke look around at each other and shake their heads no.

How do you know he's so tough?

To start with, he's strong as hell, Doug says, looking back at me through the rearview mirror. You're lucky he didn't really connect when he hit you.

Yeah, Luke says, he's the only person in school who can bench three hundred pounds.

Craig and I have a weight bench in the garage we rarely use. Once I was impressed when Craig bench-pressed two hundred and twenty.

How do you know that? I ask.

Everyone knows it, Luke says. He and Moose Johnson and Tommy Sloan had a contest once to see who was the strongest. Neither of them could get to three hundred. Jamie could.

I think he's on steroids, Kenny mutters.

He's got a scholarship to Ohio State, Doug says. He's the only kid in school who can dunk a basketball besides Stan Gabbard, and he's six-seven.

I've seen Craig dunk one, I say.

Yeah, like one out of five tries, Doug says. And that's holding it and running at the basket, not dribbling. I've seen Jamie at the park dunk it in a game. On someone. Like he's Charles-fucking-Barkley.

Jeez, Kenny says, I didn't know you had such a crush on Jamie Fergus, Doug.

Suck my dick.

I can't, Kenny says, you're too busy sucking Jamie's.

We all start laughing except for Doug.

When the laughing subsides, Luke says, You know, when we were sophomores in gym class, I saw him break someone's arm wrestling. It was gym class, not even a real match, and he twisted the kid's arm behind his back and just broke it.

Oh, yeah, I remember that, Kenny says. What was that kid's name?

I can't remember. He never came back junior year.

He was big too.

Yeah, that's why he was matched up with Fergus.

We're quiet for a minute and Luke says, You ever heard a bone break? It doesn't sound like a branch. It's something different entirely. Man, that kid looked tough, but he started screaming. I'd never heard anything like it. And his arm—the angle of it. Christ, I'm getting chills thinking of it.

Doug slows the car as he pulls into the gravel drive at the front of the junkyard. The sign says CLARKSON PARTS AND SUPPLIES. He reaches to open the door but waits.

You know, he says, Jamie wasn't always such an asshole. When we were little kids, he was all right. I think his dad really fucked him up. I remember being on the same soccer team as him when we were kids. Jamie was the star player on the team—the only reason we ever won a game—but his dad would just lay into him whenever he did anything that wasn't perfect.

I feel real sorry for him, Kenny says.

I'm just saying, Doug says. Maybe he wouldn't be such a dick if his dad didn't ride him so hard.

I don't know, Luke says. The messed up thing about the day he broke that dude's arm is that Jamie was smiling the whole time afterward. It was like he couldn't help it. He was trying to look all serious, pretend like the whole thing was an accident, but his face kept bursting into a grin.

Doug unlocks the gate and pulls in and Dawn pulls in after him. Kenny closes the gate behind us but doesn't lock it back. Doug has a key because he worked here last summer and never gave it back. He knows Davey Clarkson won't be in to work today because his dad saw him at the American Legion on Sunday getting drunk and watching football.

Doug pulls into a clearing in the middle of a labyrinth of cars and says, It's as sure as the sun rises. When he gets drunk, he spends the whole next day sleeping it off. The man has the worst hangovers. This place would have been closed twice a week in the summer if I hadn't been here.

Outside, a hint of motor oil and gasoline is in the air. And something else—some kind of decomposition.

Your brother and I spent a lot of time here, Doug says to me, when we was trying to get that Nova running.

Dawn parks her car, and Beth walks toward me smiling.

What's up, slugger? she says, giggling.

Shit, I say.

Everyone gathers around in a circle. Luke pulls out a pipe and a baggie and starts to pack the pipe. Doug leaves a door open and plays a cassette.

Luke offers the pipe to Beth. It's no bigger than my thumb, and made of marble, and she holds it to her mouth and flicks the lighter and inhales and pulls the flame into the pipe, burning the grains inside. She takes the pipe away, holding her breath, a vein standing out on her forehead, and she exhales and coughs a few times.

The faint sound of grenades and machine guns and screaming come from Doug's car. It's the opening of Metallica's "One." The guitar begins, sad and slow, and Kenny starts playing air guitar along with it. All of the girls look at him like he's weird.

Doug takes the pipe. You know, he says, the one thing I don't get is the title. Why is it called "One"?

Yeah, Kenny says, they never say the word "One" in the whole song?

Yeah they do, Luke says. There's that part where he says he's a one.

Doug coughs smoke and says, He's a *one*? That doesn't make any sense.

Yeah, Kenny says. What's that supposed to mean?

I don't know, Luke says. But I looked at the lyrics and that's what it says.

Bullshit, Doug says. I don't believe it.

Then you tell me why the song is called "One."

Luke repacks the bowl. The song is playing.

I think about not speaking up, but I do.

I think what it's supposed to mean is that, well, the song is about a guy who's lost his arms and legs, and he can't see or hear or smell or any of those things. He's completely cut off from the world. The world is gone. He's in darkness. Nothing but his own consciousness. When he says he's just one, he means he's alone.

Everyone is quiet for a moment.

Kenny frowns.

Holy shit, Dawn says, and starts laughing. This song finally makes sense to me now. I'm not kidding. I never got it before.

Jesus, Danny, Beth says, you're so smart.

I still don't think it makes any sense, Doug says. How can he be a *one*?

You're a zero, Dawn says.

Beth and I are sitting on the tailgate of an old Ford pickup truck, overlooking the junkyard, and I tell Beth that I've never felt I was like other people. I've always felt different.

She asks what I mean, and I stop and think about it for a few seconds.

I just don't think anything ever really has made me happy the way it makes other people, I say.

Beth listens. Her eyes are glassy from the pot, but she is giving me her full attention.

In front of us, Luke and Doug and Kenny are taking turns smashing the hell out of an Avenger GT with a tire iron. It's been dented up and every window has already been smashed out, but they do their best to damage it worse. The Metallica album plays out of the speakers of Doug's Ford Taurus, with its doors propped open. Dawn and Gina sit in the other car, talking and giggling.

With the cars around us—rusted and bent into unbelievable shapes, like stepped-on soda cans—it feels like we're sitting in a cemetery of car crashes, and with each car something terrible may have happened. Some cars might have been abandoned or their engines blew, and some people might have walked away from the wrecks with stiff necks or minor fractures. But some of these cars carry the weight of death. Teenagers compacted behind steering wheels, trapped in burning cars. Toddlers thrown through windshields. Pedestrians struck, their bones shattered, their muscles pulverized. Metal stretches in every direction, a labyrinth of rusting, twisted machines smelling faintly of burnt oil.

You see, I say, when I was little, I mean real little, I think I might have been normal, but once I hit about sixth grade, things started to change. I started to see the world differently. It was like I realized that the world I thought existed was just an illusion and none of what I thought was real really was.

Jesus, she says. Are you sure you didn't take a hit off that bowl?

I sit back, leaning on my hands.

Sorry, I say. I don't mean to get so serious.

It's okay.

Did that ever happen to you? Where you just start thinking about how nothing is even real. Not how we think it is anyway.

I'm not sure.

Now Kenny has the tire iron. He hauls back and whacks it against the fender, and then he drops it. It sings as it hits the dirt.

Shit, he says, shaking his hand. I didn't expect that to hurt.

It's the re-, re-, Doug starts and then stops.

Recoil? Kenny says.

Reverberations, Luke says.

Yeah, Doug says, picking up the tire iron. The vibrations. Come on, this car's toast. Let's find another one.

The sky is clear and air is cool and clouds roll forward like gray tanks toward the blue horizon.

Beth laughs. Look at us, she says. Not one of us is normal. If we were normal, we'd be at cheerleading practice or hanging out at Dairy Queen. Not sneaking into a junkyard. Getting stoned. Smashing shit.

Yeah, I say, but still, I think there's even something that separates me from—I look up and gesture toward the three guys as they find a Volkswagen Beetle and try to flip it on its side—them, I add.

Well, yeah, she says, they're idiots.

I say, It's just that, sometime around middle school, I began to think these weird thoughts that I don't think other people think. Maybe we don't really exist. Maybe the world isn't real. Life isn't what we think it is. I heard fish don't know what water is. We could be just as clueless about things in our lives too.

I'm pretty sure I exist, Beth says.

We exist, but do we matter?

Jesus, that's depressing.

The world only really exists because I perceive it. But I'm just a bag of muscles and bones that somehow work together to create electricity in my brain, allowing me to think and see and all that stuff. But really, I'm just atoms, right? Molecules and ions no different than this truck or that car those guys were beating the shit out of.

We're alive, Beth says.

Okay, but so is the grass and the trees. Are we more important than them?

We're intelligent. We have feelings.

Maybe they do too, I say, in their own way.

She frowns. Are you seriously telling me that you think grass has feelings?

I don't know. I guess not, but does it matter?

Beth sits and listens. I don't know what it is about her that makes me so comfortable telling her things like this.

I say, Imagine if aliens came down from outer space—not movie aliens, but real aliens—and they perceived the world differently than we do. Because they're aliens, they don't see and smell and all that, they see things differently—they *perceive* differently. I wonder if they could really tell the difference between us and the animals and birds and trees. Or even the cars. We're all just...I don't know what we are. But I don't think there's really much difference between me and the empty air in front of us.

But we're alive, Beth says.

Are you sure we're not just machines? We run for a while, like these cars—I gesture toward the wreckage around us—and then we stop?

No, she says. We're *alive*.

I'm quiet for a few seconds, looking out at the clouds.

What's it mean to be alive?

I say it almost in a whisper.

She starts to speak but stops.

I grin and say, I told you I didn't think like other people.

She laughs and leans toward me and bumps her shoulder against mine. I laugh with her.

You think some deep thoughts, she says.

Well, I begin, and I know I should stop but I can't help myself and I just keep talking. When you think about the world that way, I say, it just makes everything seem so insignificant, you know? When you think that you're just molecules bouncing around, just energy in a human-shaped container, and there's no heaven and no hell, and there's no such thing as a soul, and you think you're the only one in the world who thinks this way, it's hard to feel like you belong with everyone else. The people who play football and go to Boy Scouts and study for tests, like any of that matters—how do you go through life pretending to be one of those people?

We're quiet for a moment, and then we hear cheering. The guys have successfully flipped the car upside down. They high-five each other. The smiles on their faces are as big as if they'd just accomplished something great.

I thought I was the only person in the world who felt that way, I say, until my mom killed herself.

Beth is staring at me, and I feel sorry for her because she has to be tired of hearing me talk like this.

Do you still believe all that? Beth asks. About no heaven and hell and about molecules and stuff?

I don't know, I say, looking down at the ground.

There's a bolt lying in the dirt. And a washer. A shard of glass. Some other pieces of metal. Among them is a tiny plastic toy gun from a G.I. Joe action figure.

I actually do feel almost normal right now and that's what I want to tell Beth, that she makes me feel normal. Or makes me feel like I could be normal. But even with everything I'm able to say to her, I'm not sure I can say this.

Beth asks, If you believe all that, what do you think about love?

I look at her.

Well, I guess science says love is just biology. Attraction and chemicals and stuff. That's what Miss Taylor says in class.

Beth has no reaction.

But, I say, when you're falling for someone, it feels like it's gotta be more than that. It feels like maybe the soul does exist. It feels like maybe things do matter.

When you're falling for someone? she says.

Yeah, I say, and I grin.

I lean in to kiss her, and the smashed cars around us disappear and the sound of the music and the ground and the sky, and I don't know if I'm right or wrong about the world, but I know that in this moment it doesn't matter.

The sun is setting as Doug drives us toward my house. Out the window, purple clouds swell around the fire-red glow of the sun. Inside the car, everyone is quiet. Doug didn't even bother to turn on the radio. It's as if the good times at the junkyard—the laughter and the dope—couldn't hold off the real world for long, and now everyone is resigned to the idea of going home, back to their lives. Only I feel excited. Excited to have a girlfriend. And friends. And eager to get home and talk to Craig. Outside, the colors change each second. The hues in the sky look more pink. It's rare for the sky here to look anything but gray, and yet no one in the car notices but me.

Uh oh, Doug says, slowing down as we near my house.

Two police cars are parked in the driveway. Craig's Nova is not there.

Doug pulls behind one of the cruisers and puts the car in park. All three of them turn toward me, eyes wide, as if I might know what this is all about.

Only one way to find out, I say.

Call us and let us know what happened, Luke says.

Then, in case I might think this is insensitive, he adds, Your brother—let us know if he's okay.

All right, I say. I had a good time today, guys. Thanks.

We had a blast, Danny, Kenny says.

It was fun, Luke says.

Yeah, Doug says, but I still don't think you're right about "One."

I laugh and close the door. It doesn't shut tightly, so I have to open it and slam it. I turn and walk toward the house. The last color is almost gone from the sky, just a little red scar among the clouds, and the temperature seems ten degrees colder than it did when we left the junkyard.

I open the door, and all of them are standing there in the foyer: Dad and Sergeant Frederickson and two other cops, one in a uniform who I don't recognize and one out of uniform, a guy in a sport coat. It's still easy to tell he's a cop by the gun clip on his belt. I've seen him before. He came when my mom killed herself. I figure him for a detective even though I didn't know our town was big enough to need one.

All of them turn and look at me. The house is warm inside. I shut the door, but the cold lingers behind me like a fingerprint.

Hi, Danny, Sergeant Frederickson says.

Dad says, Do you know where your brother is?

I shake my head.

You sure?

The cops are looking at me. Frederickson moves his head slightly as he looks at the bruise on my cheek. Dad doesn't seem to notice.

I don't know where he is, I say.

71 —

When was the last time you saw him? the detective asks.

Why? I say.

They're the ones asking the questions, Dad says. Not you.

I saw him this morning.

Before school?

Yeah.

Your brother skipped school today, Danny, Sergeant Frederickson says. We're just trying to find out where he went.

I look one by one at each of the cops and say, I didn't know truancy was such a serious offense.

Danny, Dad snaps.

The detective speaks again. Did he mention anything about what he was going to do today? Where he might go?

I take a deep breath. He didn't say anything to me. Is someone going to tell me what the hell happened?

Each of the cops looks around at each other and then at Dad, who looks back at them.

Why don't you go to your room, Danny? Dad says without looking at me.

I walk through the house, into my room, stand for a few seconds, heart beating, and then I walk to Craig's room. I look at his bed, unmade, sheets and blanket shoved aside. I look at his pile of clothes. I look at his posters on the wall: the cover of Iron Maiden's "The Trooper" single, with the zombie soldier waving the flag; Lita Ford dressed in leather holding her guitar; a Kathy Ireland picture torn from *Sports Illustrated*, which Gretchen always hated but he refused to take down. His tapes—AC/DC and Anthrax, Sabbath and Slayer—are scattered and in disarray. It doesn't look like any are missing.

Still, I've seen the room empty a thousand times yet somehow it feels more empty than before.

I walk back toward the foyer, and Dad and the cops look at me like I'm not supposed to be there, but I stand there anyway.

Jim, Sergeant Frederickson says to my dad, if he shows up, let us know, okay?

The cops turn to leave.

This is a moment where I can stay quiet and do nothing or I can speak up and say what I want to say. I almost say nothing, but then I say, Somebody better tell me what the fuck is going on.

The uniform cop, whose hand is on the door, freezes. The others turn to look at me. Frederickson looks at the detective, and the detective nods, and Frederickson turns to me, and my dad just stares at the wall while all this is happening.

Danny, Frederickson says, the restaurant where your brother used to work was broken into last night.

Used to work? I say.

He didn't show up for his shift today, the detective says. So I'd say he's fired.

I stare at him. And you assume Craig did it?

Frederickson answers. With him not showing up to school or work or coming home yet, it's not looking good. We want to talk to him.

Bullshit, I say. You want to *talk?*

Danny, Dad hisses, and then we're all quiet, me trying to show them my rage and contain it all at the same time.

What did this burglar make off with? I ask. Hamburgers and hot dogs?

It's quite a bit more serious than that.

I feel the money in my jacket pocket. I feel like they can see it too, sagging my jacket down on the one side like a ten-pound weight.

Frederickson looks at me with the same I-want-what's-best-for-you expression I've seen before and says, Danny, if you hear from your brother, it's important that you let us know. And it's important that you tell him to come home. If he stays gone this is liable to get a whole lot worse. Understand?

I say nothing.

You've got my number, Danny.

I turn away and walk to my room. I look for a cassette to play, something heavy to blast so the police will hear it, and I realize I never told them that Craig didn't do it. I never defended him. Even though I know he did it, I should have said Craig would never do such a thing and that they should look for someone else. *Then* I should have walked away.

I walk quickly back down the hall so I can say this to them, but the police have already left. Dad is in the kitchen, leaning into the refrigerator for a beer.

Shit, I say.

What?

Nothing.

Dad shakes his head, as if in disapproval.

Now I say, What?

That brother of yours, he says, and he takes a long drink.

What about him?

He ain't worth a damn.

He didn't do this, I say.

Dad ignores me. I hope he doesn't come back. We're better off without him.

I walk away, slam my door, and blast "Parental Guidance" by Judas Priest so Dad can hear it. But the song is too tame, too soft. Ultimately, it's about finding common ground with your parents, so I have to turn it off before the last verse. I play "Institutionalized" by Suicidal Tendencies, but that's not quite right either, so I stop it halfway through. I try "Dyers Eve" by Metallica, and it's fast and angry and I listen to the whole song, but it's about parents sheltering kids so that they are surprised by the horrors of the world when they grow up. So that's not how I'm feeling either. When the song is over, I lie on my bed and stare at the ceiling in silence, and I think about if I tried to express my rage at the world what my song would sound like.

The phone rings. It must be Craig or some news of Craig. I continue to lie on my back, staring at the ceiling. I listen. Dad answers. I hear him say hang on. His voice sounds a little disappointed, confused. I hear him coming down the hall. He knocks on my door, pushes it open, and says, Danny, It's for you.

I sit up.

I act as if this is normal: me getting phone calls.

His face gives no indication who it might be.

I follow him down the hall and answer. It's Beth.

Hey, I say, softly, standing in the living room, knowing my dad is listening in his chair with a cigarette and a beer.

I heard the cops came by, Beth says. What happened?

Nothing, I say. Hang on.

I pick up the phone and pull the cord down the hall the way Craig used to do when he talked with Gretchen for hours at a time. I stretch it as far as it will go, but my room is farther down the hall and the cord won't stretch that far. I sit in the hall, leaning my back against the wall, my knees an inverted V. The sound of Dad's TV plays from the living room.

Okay, I say. I'm back.

Is everything okay?

I don't know how much to tell her. I've been honest with her about so many things I never would have told anyone, but we're talking about Craig now and I don't want to tell her anything. I don't want to tell her what the police wanted. I don't want to tell her that the restaurant was broken into. I don't want to tell her that Craig is gone. I don't want to explain that there was something different about this morning, the way he was with me, that I couldn't tell it at the time, but now I can see it.

But there are some things I have to say, facts that she'll find out anyway.

Danny?

Yeah, I say, just trying to think where to begin.

She waits and the phone is silent. A commercial for NyQuil is playing in the living room, and the voice says it's now in Cherry flavor. I think of red cough syrup, and it makes me think of the sticky consistency of Mom's blood.

I guess the restaurant where Craig works was broken into last night, I say.

Oh.

And Craig ditched school today and hasn't come home, so I guess they think he might be a suspect.

What do you think?

I think they're just looking for the easiest person to blame, I say.

Yeah. Dickhead cops.

We talk for an hour more, about everything and about nothing, and then Dad comes walking down the hall and says, Craig's gone and now you're gonna start doing this shit? It's late, Danny.

I say nothing.

He goes into the bathroom and urinates. The TV is off, which means he is going to bed. I stand and walk back to the living room.

I should go, I say.

Me too, Beth says.

We say goodnight, and it seems like she wants to linger on the phone, but I want to get off the line. Now that Dad is in bed, there's something I need to do.

When I hang up, I look down the hall and make sure Dad's door is closed. It is. I go to the gun cabinet and look inside. The Magnum is there. It sits in the bottom of the cabinet among the ammunition boxes, right where I left it.

I check to make sure the other guns are there, but there's no way Craig would have taken a rifle or a shotgun.

It occurs to me: there's one more I didn't think of. Dad's .38 he keeps on the floor under his bed.

I sit up for a while watching TV with the volume turned low. MTV videos. U2. Tom Petty. Debbie Gibson. Whitney Houston. I'm thinking the whole time, only partly paying attention. When the song "Don't Worry, Be Happy" comes on, I turn the TV off. I walk quietly down the hall. I open Dad's door. Everything is dark, but I can see shapes. I know my way. I see the dresser and the bed, and Dad's shape in it. I hear him snoring. He sounds like an animal.

I walk forward. One step and stop. Then another. I kneel onto the floor. Hands and knees. I'm next to the bed, reaching under. His breathing is loud. I can't find the gun. My hand grasps in the dark, but the gun's not there. I flatten my palm against the carpet, the newest carpet in the house because it had to be replaced because Mom's blood was all over the room. I slide my hand around, wide swaths. The gun is gone. The gun is gone.

I rise up and walk toward the door. I collide loudly with something. Mom's cedar chest.

Danny!

It's just me, I say. Go back to sleep.

What are you doing?

Nothing. I'm at the door now, closing it behind me. Go back to sleep, Dad.

I'm hurrying down the hall, but he opens the door.

— 76

Stop!

I lean against the wall and wait, my head down, not looking.

What the hell? he says, walking toward me.

He's wearing underwear and a tee shirt and nothing else.

I couldn't find my headphones. I thought maybe you had them.

I know it's preposterous as soon as I say it.

Now he's facing me. Danny, he says, his voice a growl. Don't you fucking lie to me.

I look up and stare at his eyes. He stares back, and his anger bores into me like a drill.

I was looking for your gun, okay?

He squints at me as if he's trying to see past me to some understanding of what this could mean.

To see if Craig took it, I say.

Why would he take—

Because he's not coming back, I say, and I turn away from him and go into my room and close my door behind me.

With my clothes still on, I pull the covers over me. Faintly, I hear the suction sound of the refrigerator door, then the thud of it closing, the pop-snap of a beer opening, and finally the TV turned low. But it's all very far away and through a muffled fog.

It's as if I've known all day, and I chose to ignore what I knew. And when the police were here, finally I couldn't ignore it any longer. But I wanted confirmation. And now I have it. And now that I can't pretend anymore, some type of button has been pushed inside of me. Some emotional lever has been pulled. But the lever didn't get moved to sadness or anger or guilt or any of those gears. It's stuck in numbness. And I fall asleep in the fog of that numbness.

Dad and I get ready in the morning like everything is normal. We don't speak. I eat breakfast while he watches the morning news and smokes. I take a shower and let the hot water run over my body. The house is cold, so I stand under the spray for a long time, turning, moving my neck, letting the steam rise around me. I open my mouth, let the warm water fill it, and then spit. The water starts to turn cold.

As I walk through the house in a towel, Dad says, You were in there long enough. How was she?

I ignore him.

After Dad leaves for work but before the bus comes, I walk into Craig's room and look around.

I used to come in here a lot, just to hang out. Craig would be listening to music, and I would come in and we'd sit on the bed and talk or not talk, just be in the same place together. Everything I am—all my interests and tastes—is because of him. If he'd listened to country music or liked to watch sports, I would have done those things. But he didn't, so I didn't.

We have the same interests, but we are different. I'm quiet and don't fit in, and he has such an easy way about him, able to make friends and talk to people. It's not that he's all that friendly. People want him to like them even though he doesn't much care what they think of him. He's a sun and most people are planets. Adults always seem to think I've got my head on straight and he's the fuck-up. I think even he thinks that. But that's because he has a hair-trigger temper. There's rage boiling inside him all the time, like magma bubbling inside a volcano. People don't see that there's something else in me, something worse, something sicker.

The night after the funeral, I was lying in bed, twisting around in the sheets, sweating and breathing fast and having fits of sobbing. I pulled on my hair and punched myself in the leg and the stomach and slapped my face, but I couldn't get out of my head what she looked like when I found her. I walked in here into Craig's room, and I crawled into bed with him, like a little kid getting into bed with his parents after having a nightmare. I curled into a ball and started crying, and Craig rolled over, put his arm around me, and started singing to me, softly like Mom did when I was really little. He sang the Judas Priest song "Out in the Cold," which I always thought was a breakup song but the lyrics work for a dead mom too. It's a slow song, as Judas Priest songs go, and he sang it like a lullaby. I cried harder at first, but then I calmed down. It was something I needed, to cry and be comforted. I finally fell asleep and—for the first time since I found her—didn't have nightmares.

When people talk about Craig like he's no good, I want them to see moments like that.

His room is the same as it was the day before. He left it as if he was coming back. There's no evidence of a packed bag. Did he take even one change of clothes?

Still, I know he is gone.

Part of me wants him to come back. But that would make what he's doing—taking off—turn out to be a failure. And I don't want my brother to fail. I want him to succeed. I want him to run away and never come back. I could carry that with pride. The way people would talk about it: Danny's brother, he just up and took off. Robbed the restaurant and took off, never to be seen again.

But if he comes back, in a week or in a month, he'll come back in shame, and I don't want that for him. He'll be the fuck-up everyone expects him to be. Now that he's gone, he has to stay gone.

I sit on the edge of the bed, but then I stand because I don't want to mess it up. I want to leave it as is.

The room smells of him.

I know roughly how long it will take the smell to fade because I know how long it took for the house to stop smelling like Mom.

Beth comes to find me at my locker. Today she is wearing a Whitesnake tee shirt, and her hair is pulled back and braided, which is different and very pretty. Her face seems to stand out somehow, and her eyes pop—a rich apple green framed by her dark eye shadow. She is smiling, and I smile back, and I almost forget that my brother is gone.

She hugs me. Then we kiss. And it's natural. Like this is what we do now.

She asks if there's any word from Craig. I shake my head no. I reach into my locker and get my book for first period. I try to think of what to ask her because it seems like our conversations are always about me, about my mom, or my brother, or some other part of my screwed-up life.

I close my locker and lean against it and get ready to ask Beth how things are with her stepdad, but over her shoulder I see Gretchen walking toward us. I expect Jamie Fergus to be with her, but he isn't. She is walking directly toward me. I pretend I don't notice her.

She stands next to us, waiting for me to look.

Beth says, Hi, Gretchen.

Can I talk to you, Danny?

About what?

I just want to talk.

Beth says, I'll see you later, Danny.

I don't want her to go, but she's gone before I can say anything.

Gretchen is at least eight inches shorter than me but somehow I feel small. Beth can't compare to how pretty she is, and I feel guilty for noticing this, but it's true. Her skin—somehow supernaturally smooth like she's never had a blemish in her life—seems to glow, as if sunlight is underneath, shining from inside her. And her hair, so blonde it looks like it's been colored with a yellow crayon, hangs around her shoulders with every curl in place, not glued there with hairspray like every other girl in school but natural and loose and effortless. She looks as if she wakes up in the morning and comes out of a package, perfect and beautiful, and I always wanted her to make an effort to get to know me because I'm shy and quiet and I needed her to be the one to take the initiative. But she never would. She ignored me, and when Craig was with her, he ignored me too.

You and your brother sure got yourself into a mess, she says.

Her cheeks are flushed, but it only makes her prettier. Vulnerable almost. What mess?

Danny, don't play stupid.

I look around. The other kids are watching us. Gretchen turns. What the fuck are you looking at, Sally? she says.

Excuse me for living, Sally Parker says, closing her locker and spinning on her heels. The other students turn.

The first bell rings, telling us we have only two minutes before class.

Gretchen, what do you want from me?

I want you and your brother to stay away from Jamie, so no one gets hurt. He's going to kill the both of you if you don't lay off.

Lay off?

Yeah, Craig started this shit.

And what exactly did I do?

You spit on him, didn't you?

The halls are clearing out. We're almost alone.

He had that coming, I say quietly.

She rolls her eyes.

Men, she says. All this male bravado.

That's a big word for you.

I'm not a retard, Danny.

I take a deep breath. I speak calmly. You're a tough girl, Gretchen. You don't let anyone push you around. Why don't you talk to him instead of talking to me?

I can't talk to Craig. You saw what happened—

Not Craig. Your boyfriend.

Jamie?

I tell her if she doesn't want things to get further out of hand, she should be talking to Jamie Fergus, trying to make peace between all of us that way. She never seemed to have any trouble making Craig walk the line—as that country singer my dad likes would say—so I imply without coming right out and saying that she should do the same to Jamie.

She's quiet, and the bell rings. We're alone in the hall, and the expression on her face tells me something. She doesn't treat Jamie like she treated Craig. She could boss Craig around sometimes, and sometimes he would let her. Not all the time. That was why they didn't work—they would fight. They seemed too much alike. Mostly it seemed like Gretchen would win. She was in control. It was when Craig started to put up more of a fight that things fell apart. But I can see on her face that Jamie is different. Jamie's the boss.

Her pleading eyes tell me that she's ashamed of this.

She shakes her head, looks away, looks back.

Just tell your brother to stay away from Jamie for a while.

She smiles at me, and that one smile makes me want to like her and to do what she wants, and at the same time it makes me hate her for how pretty she is. It's not right that someone should be so pretty that it just erases everything else about her.

Craig's gone, I say.

She looks surprised. There's something else in her expression too. She's awestruck, like she didn't know he had it in him.

What do you mean gone?

He left, I say. For good.

Her expression changes again, as the impressed part of her turns doubtful. He'll be back, she says.

I've got to go to class.

Wait, she says, and she reaches out and touches my arm.

She's trying to charm me, like a vampire luring a victim into its lair.

You know why I broke up with Craig?

I don't move.

It became too hard, Danny. It was too much work. Everything was always about him and his pain. He just never seemed to be able to...I don't know...*adjust*.

I want to tell her that I saw him buy her flowers, that he would talk about the cheerleading squad because she was on it, that I never thought he was focusing on himself, that I always thought he put her first.

You know, Gretchen says, it seemed like you handled your mother's death so much better than your brother did. You were always so levelheaded about the whole thing. But Craig...I wanted to help him, but eventually I just had to do what was right for me. You know?

She stares at me, shrugging her shoulders, giving me a look that I'm sure always gets its way. I'm sure it did with Craig. I'm sure it does with her parents. Probably even with Jamie, some of the time anyway.

Gretchen, I say. You don't know me at all. And I don't know you. And I don't think you know Craig.

I want to add, Because Craig *handled* Mom's death a lot better than I did, but I don't.

Oh, I *know* Craig, she says. Too well.

Well, I don't think he ever really knew you.

She looks at me like I slapped her.

If you think I'm such a bitch, Danny, what was that all about the other night? Why not just let your brother blow my brains out? Not that he ever would have gone through with it.

I start to say that she shouldn't be too sure of herself, but I stop myself. I say, I wasn't protecting *you*, Gretchen.

She opens her mouth to speak, then closes it. And then Mrs. O'Rourke, the librarian, walks around the corner and sees us.

Aren't you two supposed to be in class? she says.

I was just coming to the library to see you, Gretchen says.

Do you have a pass?

No, Mr. Staub couldn't find his, but he said it would be okay if I just explained to you what I was doing.

Mrs. O'Rourke, who is young and plump and friendly, thinks about this for a moment, skeptical at first, and then Gretchen's magic takes its effect. Her face changes and, although she doesn't say anything, it's clear she's going to accept this explanation. She turns to me.

And you? she says.

Oh, he was just heading to the office, Gretchen says. Don't worry, she says to me, putting her hand on my shoulder. I don't think they'll count you tardy. Diarrhea is a valid excuse.

Mrs. O'Rourke looks back and forth between us, red blooming on her cheeks like a rose.

I put my hand on Gretchen's shoulder. And you shouldn't worry, I say. I'm sure Mrs. O'Rourke can help you find a book on teenage pregnancy.

Gretchen flinches.

Before she can say anything else, I turn and walk down the hallway.

The vice principal assigns me detention for being late again. But she is nice about it, and I'm glad I don't have to listen to Mr. Kerr lecture me about caring.

First period goes by in a blur. In study hall, I get another slip to go see the guidance counselor.

Mr. James is reading a book when I walk in. He quickly closes it and turns it cover down on the desk. The title on the spine is upside down, but I can tell it says *Preventing Teenage Suicide*.

I got another one of these, I say, holding up the slip of paper Mrs. McCreary gave me.

Yes, he says, please sit down.

I sit and say, Two days in a row, huh?

Well, he says, I didn't really like how we left things yesterday. And it seems like you've had an eventful twenty-four hours.

I don't speak.

He's quiet too, waiting for me to say something. Finally, he says, Since I saw you yesterday, you got in a fight and your brother's gone missing, right?

I take a deep breath. I look around the room. I stare at a poster of a lake with a low-lying mist hanging over it, pink from sunrise. The accompanying quotation says,

A straight oar looks bent in the water.
What matters is not merely that we see things but how we see them.
—Michel de Montaigne

I don't know who that is.

Talk to me, Danny, he says. Tell me what's going on.

I look at him. I think. I shake my head a little and say, I don't want to do this today.

He stares at me.

I start to rise out of my chair.

Wait, he says.

I sit back down.

Danny, I'm just going to take the direct approach. I want to know if you think about suicide.

My heart is pounding. The blood pumping through my veins must be affecting my vision because Mr. James looks as if he's in a long tunnel where everything else is blurry and only he is in focus.

I'm worried about you, Danny. We've talked around this for I don't know how long, but I think now it's time to address it head on.

I think about what Craig would do if he were here and that gives me the strength to stand and say, I just want everyone to leave me alone. Why can't you do that?

I wanted my voice to sound strong, like Craig's, but when it comes out I can hear myself in the request—the pleading agony.

Mr. James exhales like he's been gut-punched.

I turn to go because I'm committed now.

In the hallway, he calls to me: Danny, wait!

He approaches me, and he's out of breath like he just ran a long way, but he didn't.

Listen, he says. You've got to be able to ask for help.

He stares at me, and even though I won the staring contest with Jamie Fergus yesterday, I can't with him. I look down at the floor. I look at my shoes. They are dirty, with holes, with the strings tied together in places where they've broken.

I'm offering to help, Danny. It doesn't have to be me, but you have to let someone help you.

I'm fine, I say.

Maybe you are, he says, but *if* you have suicidal thoughts, you need to be willing to let someone help you.

I lean against the lockers. I look down one side of the hallway and then the other. No one else is around.

I don't want to be manipulative by bringing up your mother, he says, and I hope I'm not going too far, but wouldn't you have wanted her to ask for help? Wouldn't you—

That *is* going too far! I snap, staring at him with the same burning anger I used in my eyes against Jamie yesterday.

He stops and then gently says, I'm sorry, Danny, I'm just—

Why the fuck do you care so much anyway? Fucking faggot!

He says nothing, and the silence seems to fill the void between us like a physical shape. I walk away. I want to punch my fist into a locker—that's what Craig would do—but I hold the anger inside.

I'm in the lunch line with Dawn and Kenny, waiting for Beth. Dawn is complaining about a pop quiz in Government class, saying how the hell should she know what political party Ronald Reagan is a member of.

Kenny's eyes glance over my shoulder. He opens his mouth to warn me, but then I feel a slap on my shoulder.

Hey, little boy, Jamie Fergus says.

He is smiling, like we are pals. He is here with two of his golems. The bruise around his eye is starting to fade, but the yellow skin looks almost greenish, like he's beginning to rot from his eye socket.

I say nothing.

Where's your big brother today?

I don't answer.

You got nothing to say to that? Don't want your brother to get hurt, is that it?

I can't think of anything to say to this and so I say nothing, but still I'm staring and my eyes aren't blinking.

Jamie, Dawn says, why don't you leave the kid alone? Stop being such a dickhead.

Hey, he says, putting his arms up in innocence. My fight isn't with him. It's with his brother.

People have gathered in a crowd, like yesterday.

I don't see my brother, I say, holding my hands up and looking around. Do you?

Kid, are you fucking retarded?

Are you?

He steps forward, puffing out his chest.

Every word you say makes the pounding your brother is going to get worse, he says loudly.

His face is so close I can smell his breath. His eyes, I notice for the first time, are an aqua blue, and I can see why the girls like him.

I smirk and say, quietly, so only he and those closest to us can hear, Do you think they'll let you keep your football scholarship if you're in a wheelchair?

He pulls back an inch or two. He narrows his eyes and stares at me.

Are you fucking threatening me? he says.

Mr. Delaney and Mr. Kerr and Mr. Bell are pushing through the students, trying to get to us.

Think about this, I say to Jamie, still speaking softly. What have you got to lose and what have we got to lose? That's the only question you should be thinking about.

His skin seems white and his mouth is open, and he looks scared. I don't know if anyone has ever seen him like this, but the expression is there, for a moment. Mr. Kerr shoves himself between us, one hand on each of our chests. Jamie's face is back to normal, a mask of confidence.

What's going on? Mr. Kerr says.

Nothing, Jamie says.

Kerr looks at me.

I say nothing.

The other teachers are there, and the crowd is still around us, wondering what's going to happen.

Let's go to the office, you two, Mr. Bell says.

I'm hungry, I say. I'm going to eat my lunch.

I take a step away, but Mr. Kerr yells at me to wait.

I want to know what the hell was going on here.

We were talking, I say.

Talking? Then what's this crowd doing here?

You'll have to ask them.

I walk away. Everyone is watching me, but I don't see any of them. I just move through them like they're phantoms in fog.

Beth comes through the crowd and she's real, something solid in a sea of smoke, and I grab her hand and say, I can't take this place today. You want to get out of here?

We walk down the hall and push through the side door by Poplar Street, the one people use sometimes to sneak cigarette breaks. Cutting through the brown grass, we head toward the nearby neighborhood. The wind is cold, but as it pushes my hair back, I love the way it feels on my face. I'm never outside this time of day. Beth is smiling. We are holding hands.

Let's go to my house, she says. No one's home.

Her duplex is warm and empty, and it feels different somehow from when I was here before. It feels like her house now, not her mom's house. She puts a Wendy O. Williams' cassette on from her bedroom and turns it up loud so we can hear it in the living room. The raspy voice starts singing about how she loves sex and rock and roll.

Beth comes out of the bedroom and jumps on the couch and runs in place, pumping her fists in the air. She yells.

It feels so fucking good to be out of there!

I'm smiling.

She jumps down and runs to the refrigerator.

Want a beer? she says. There's almost a case in here. My mom's asshole boyfriend won't miss a couple.

She brings me one, and I take a drink. Beth does too. We smile at each other and laugh. She sets her beer down on the table and takes mine and sets it down too. She grabs me by the jacket and pulls me into her, and we're kissing, mouths and tongues, our bodies pressing into each other with urgency like we might never get this chance again. I hold onto her as tight as I can, my mouth opening and closing, my tongue reaching out to hers. With our bodies pressed so tightly, I'm sure she can feel my erection, like a statue in my jeans.

Come on, she says, pulling me by the hand.

I follow her to the bedroom. She turns down the music, and then she's on top of me, on the bed, pulling off her shirt. Her breasts are large in a light-blue bra.

You don't have a condom, do you? she says, reaching behind her back with both hands and unclasping her bra.

No.

We can't do it, she says. I can't get pregnant.

Okay.

But we can mess around, she says, lowering her breasts toward my face—her nipples large and round and red—where I grab them and massage them with my hands. I've never touched breasts before and they feel different than I expected.

She pulls my shirt off over my head and starts tracing her fingers over my chest. Then she's kissing me, straddling me, my hands on her skin and in her hair, our bare chests pressed against each other, holding each other so close it's like we're trying to never let go.

We lie naked under the covers, heads sharing her pillow, looking at the ceiling. The cassette has stopped playing. Down the hall, the phone starts ringing. It rings five times before the answering machine picks up. No one leaves a message.

Can you believe we'd be in final period right now? Beth says.

I pause and then I say, No.

She starts laughing.

What? I say.

It's just that you thought about it awfully hard, she says. You gave it some serious thought. You're so cute, Danny.

I smile because I don't know what to say. I did think about her question because it feels strange to not only be out of school right now, it feels like I've left my own life. I have a new life now, and that's what feels weird: ordinarily, at this time of day, I would be in my old life.

I reach underneath the covers and put my fingers on her skin. I move the fingertips in circles, touching the softness. I pull the sheet down slowly, over the mound of her breasts, past her nipples, and down to her waist. My fingers resume their play, tracing circles and figure eights.

I say, I can't believe how lucky I am to get to touch you.

Her expression changes, and I think I've said the wrong thing and hurt her feelings. My fingers stop.

What's wrong? I say.

Nothing, she says. It's just that might be the nicest thing anyone's ever said to me.

We hug and hold each other and stay like that for several minutes. I breathe her in and out and don't think about anything else.

Later, we sit up and lean against pillows and talk. I ask questions, and for a while Beth seems really happy to chat about growing up and who her friends were and what she liked to do when she was a little kid. She went to the other elementary school and middle school in town, so that's why I never knew her growing up. She tells me about the cartoons she used to watch after school—*Inspector Gadget* and *Jem*—and how her favorite movie is *The Lost Boys*. She tells me about her first kiss and how his mouth tasted like peanut butter. I can't believe how jealous I am hearing her talk about it, how I feel sick inside. I assume she's had sex before, and I'm just glad she doesn't talk about any boys besides that awkward first kiss in sixth grade.

She says she has only one memory of her father. It was summer, and he was holding her hands and swinging her in circles, her bare feet tickled by high grass as he swooped her around and around, laughing. She wasn't scared because she knew he wouldn't let go. She doesn't understand how she can have such a sweet memory of a man who left them when she was four. She wants to remember bad things about him but can't.

Beth says it took a while growing up before she realized how poor they were compared to some of the kids in town.

You know, she says, I always tell myself that life is going to get better, that I just have to wait things out.

Her eyes look sad and exposed, like she's pulled off a mask. How strange it is that we can do that, just let our emotions out and then we look completely different. Nothing physical changes in our faces, but we expose ourselves, what's underneath. My mom always looked sad but I don't think I ever saw what was underneath. She never completely took off the mask. It's tempting to think that her expression when she was dead was her true self, but I know it's not—she was gone by then. When the blood came exploding out the back of her skull, she went with it, vanishing like a wisp of mist.

Beth looks beautiful without her mask on—the prettiest I've ever seen her.

She says, I just think to myself that life will be better when I'm an adult, when I'm out of high school.

The blankets are pulled up over us, balled and in disarray. Our feet poke out the bottom into the chill of the room. Under the covers, Beth's warmth emanates from her like she's a sun.

Beth keeps talking, saying she's been thinking about what I said at the junkyard about growing up. She talks about how there was a time in her life, when she was younger, when she was very happy. She got good grades, she had friends she really liked, she saw nothing wrong with living alone with her mom. And then somehow things started to change. It was as if suddenly her eyes were changing and she was able to see the world differently.

Kind of like you were saying, she says, only not so weird.

She giggles at this, and I smile.

She says she saw that some girls were mean. And that some people had more money and wore better clothes. And the things that used to bring her happiness no longer did. She couldn't go out for cheerleading. She couldn't play volleyball. It was as if, once she saw the world for what it was, the world kept changing to become what she expected it to be, fulfilling the prophecy of her mind. Her mom started dating Jared and that was the ultimate example. The only person who had ever really been there for her—her mom—was dating some dickhead she met at a bar. It was a betrayal—the world had finally turned against her completely.

The first time I heard them fucking, Beth says, I sat in here and almost started screaming. They were trying to be quiet, but the walls are thin and I could hear my mom moaning a little, the bed squeaking just a tiny bit.

I grabbed my hair like this, she adds, balling her fists into her hair, and I pulled. I opened my mouth like I was yelling but I stopped myself from letting any noise come out.

I listen to Beth and watch her, noticing every freckle, every blemish, every imperfection that makes her perfect.

I think I was like thirteen at the time, she says. But I decided that I just had to wait. I just had to wait out the rest of my childhood and somehow get through it. It's that simple.

Simple, I say.

Yeah, really. It's like a prison sentence. You've got a parole date in five or so years. Life will start to get better. You have to make the best of it until then. But someday life will be better and you won't have to work at it. That's what I think.

She is smiling, and I see in her eyes that she believes in this plan. She has carefully worked out this philosophy.

What if life doesn't get better? I say.

It has to, she says.

I look away from her.

I don't know, I say. Think about our parents. My dad goes to work, comes home, drinks beer in front of the TV, and then repeats the whole thing the next day. Would you trade places with your mom? Would you want that life?

Yeah, but we're not like them, she says. We won't make the same mistakes. Plenty of people their age have really kick-ass lives. No way, she says. I'm not turning into my mom.

She's smiling and confident again.

And you won't turn into your dad, she adds.

Yeah, I know.

I don't want to tell her it isn't my dad I'm afraid of turning into.

Beth rises to go to the bathroom and she walks naked across the room. Her skin is like buttermilk, and she is voluptuous and curvy. There are pockets of flab, on her butt and on her sides, but she is real and not some model in a magazine, and I think she's sexy. She is not self-conscious about walking in front of me in the nude.

Don't go anywhere, she says.

She walks out of the room and into the house, leaving the door open.

I lie back in bed and stare at the ceiling and wonder how my life could have gotten so good so fast. And then I think about Jamie Fergus and leaving school early and Craig, missing, and I tell myself to stop thinking about these things and just think about Beth and her milky-white skin. Pretend that life is good because, right now, in this moment, it is.

I hear a noise out in the house. I assume it's Beth, but then I hear heals clicking on the tile entry floor and car keys being dropped on the kitchen table.

I jump out of bed and pull on my jeans, ignoring my underwear. My shirt is an inside-out mess from when Beth pulled it off of me, and I've got my arm in one sleeve but the rest is too tangled for me to find the head hole.

Beth! I hear down the hall. What in the—

I came home sick, Beth says quickly. I was sleeping. Wait! Mom!

I drop to the floor beside the bed and start to slide under, but it's narrow and I barely fit. I hear the footsteps, and I stop moving. I see Beth's mom's feet from under the bed. I can feel her scanning the room, looking for clues. One of my shoes is over by her feet, but it's half hidden behind the open door. If she took a few steps into the room, she'd see me, halfway under the bed, my shirt only partway on.

Beth rushes past her, storming into the room. She walks just within my line of sight and grabs a robe off the top of her clothes hamper and swings it around her like a cape.

I was sick, Beth says, tying the front of her robe. I came home early.

Bullshit, her mom says.

Bull true.

I try to control my breathing because from where I am it sounds loud.

There's a long pause and I hear Beth's mom say that the school is supposed to call if you go home sick. Beth tells her that she felt so bad she didn't want to deal with the nurse and calling her.

If you're sick, why are you running around the house naked?

I was sleeping.

You sleep in the nude?

Sometimes.

I've never seen you.

Mom, Beth says, exasperated, what's the big deal?

Don't take that tone with me.

Beth says nothing.

The big deal, her mom says, is that they said a boy was ditching too. It sounded like that boy you had over here the other day.

Danny?

Yeah, Danny. And I come home and you're gallivanting around the house in your birthday suit. I'm half afraid to look under your bed or in your closet.

Beth rolls her eyes. Give me a break, she says.

There is a long period of silence. Beth stares at her mom and I feel her mom staring back.

You're grounded, young lady.

Beth glares at her. I know she would argue, but she doesn't want to continue the conversation. She wants her mom out of her room. But her silence is an admission of sorts, and so when Beth doesn't respond, her mom turns and walks from the room. Beth closes the door behind her and locks it. She turns the lock slowly, trying to do it quietly, but I hear it and I bet her mom hears it too.

I'm still on the floor, partway under the bed, and Beth stands over me and puts her finger to her mouth and whispers, Shhh. She walks over to her radio and plays the tape. She turns the volume about halfway up, loud enough to cover any noise we make but not loud enough that her mom will come back and pound on the door.

I rise silently and Beth kisses me and says, You've gotta get out of here.

She is smiling, but there's an underlying anxiety behind it.

I fix my shirt and put it on right, and I sit on the edge of the bed, tying my shoes. Beth goes to the window and opens the blind and tries to ease the window open. She tries to do it quietly, but when the lower sash breaks free from being locked in place all winter, it's so loud it sounds like she punched the wall. She looks at me and we both freeze. She slides it the rest of the way up and does the same to the storm window, which screeches like a rusty fence gate. Cold air rushes into the room.

Beth kisses me quickly and whispers that she'll see me tomorrow.

I had a great time, she says.

Me too, I say.

I kiss her again, this time for a long time, with our tongues curling around each other. And then I boost myself up and out the window.

The sky is cloud-covered from horizon to horizon, a hazy shade of light gray with wrinkles of purple and dark blue. The sun, lowering in the west, is a smudge of color behind the gray. Its shine is so dulled by the clouds that it looks more like an orange moon.

I walk through Beth's neighborhood and through town, my hands stuffed in my jacket pockets, my head held high against the cold. The walk is going by in a blur. My mind is so busy thinking about Beth that before I know it I'm to a field, taking the shortcut, and then I'm walking through the frozen, clumpy ground. My feet are floating above the soil and time is going by fast.

I'm coming up on a dirt road that runs between two fields, a couple miles from my house. There's a clearing back at the edge of a wood with mounds of dirt and a rusted backhoe sitting petrified like an old metal dinosaur. The tires are huge, almost as tall as me, with cracks in the rubber like wrinkles in an elephant's skin. When I was little, Craig and I snuck out here to play. I stop and stand and look at the backhoe, frozen in place just as it was then. I see us playing on the hills of dirt, climbing onto the backhoe. I see it like I'm watching a movie, and I'm a character in that movie.

The young version of me climbs up into the seat—cracked with foam stuffing coming out of the fissures—and puts his hands on the large steering wheel. I pretend to work the gears and make noises with my mouth like a revving engine. I am ten and Craig is fourteen. He is too old to be playing but he does it for me. We pretend we're in a post-apocalyptic world. I'm Mad Max, fleeing a gang riding motorcycles and armored muscle cars. Craig pretends to be the gang members, leaping from imagined vehicles and climbing onto the backhoe. I kick him off, then smash his car with the backhoe's claw, knock another off the road with the bucket. The grass disappears, and in the fantasy the stationary backhoe is flying down a desert highway. The apocalypse is adventure. In this time, Mom is home, lying in the dark, and neither of us knows that we will live through a real apocalypse, and it will be nothing like the movies, nothing like the games we played.

I walk up the dirt road between the two fields to the highway where I always cross over to the street my house is on. Cars go by. One approaching on the highway is a red Camaro. This pulls me out of my daze. I stop and wait.

The Camaro looks like Jamie's and it's not a hundred feet away. There are two shapes behind the windows and I know who they are.

I think they don't see me.

But when the car is right in line with me, Jamie is staring at me.

After the Camaro passes, I start moving again. I get to the fence and climb it, careful not to let the barbed wire snag my jeans. I cross the ditch, look down the highway, to the north and to the south, and when there is a break in the cars, I cross. In the middle of the road, I see the red hulk of Jamie's car, far away but coming back.

I head down the street I live on, walking on the gravel shoulder. To my right are houses, but there's no sign of anyone in the yards or driveways. To my left, on the other side of the road, is another field, plowed clean for the winter. My house is a mile ahead.

I glance back once and Jamie's car is turning onto the road, blood red and squatting on big tires low to the ground, like a predator stalking after its prey.

I step farther onto the shoulder, halfway down into the ditch, and I keep walking. I don't turn around. I expect him to come roaring past, trying to show off. Instead the Camaro comes rumbling up slowly, its engine a low growl, and creeps along next to me.

Gretchen is in the passenger seat and her window is rolled down.

Hey, Jamie calls across her.

I turn but I don't stop walking.

Want a ride, kid?

Gretchen says, Jamie, just leave him alone.

I'm just trying to help.

I face forward and walk, my hands in my pockets.

You walk home every day? he asks.

Let's just go, Gretchen says.

A car passes Jamie and honks its horn.

Fuck you, Jamie shouts.

The car speeds ahead of us. I keep walking. I don't turn my head.

Hey, kid.

I don't respond.

Hey, kid.

I walk. The car rumbles.

You don't want me to stop this car.

Come on, Gretchen says to Jamie. Just leave him alone, all right?

I just want to talk and he won't talk to me. Hey, he says, louder now. Pussy! I'm talking to you.

I don't turn. I don't say anything.

Another car pulls around Jamie. I'm still not close enough to see my house. I keep looking and walking and waiting for it to come into view. I'm hoping that Craig's Nova will be sitting in the driveway.

Jamie hits the brakes. I walk past, but hear him shift into park.

I'm going to kick this kid's—

Just leave him alone, Gretchen says, loud, her voice pleading.

I don't speed up. I don't turn back. I walk as if they're not there. If Jamie and Gretchen were speaking, I would hear them, but they aren't saying anything.

I must be thirty feet past them.

Then the wheels are spinning, screeching, and I hear the car coming but I don't turn. One set of wheels crunches the gravel shoulder, and now the car is beside me, sloping down the bank of the ditch, the mirror only half a foot from hitting my arm. Gravel sprays against my pant leg.

The Camaro passes me, its rear tire sliding farther into the ditch— clawing up a brown trench in the weeds—as he steers the front onto the pavement. The air is clouded with exhaust and rubber-smoke.

I walk over the tire scar and know that if he had turned the wheel a second sooner he would have hit me.

I step out of the ditch and keep walking and wait for my heart to stop pounding.

When I walk into the house, I expect to see Mom sitting at the kitchen table. It still happens—thinking I'll see her in familiar places. I wonder if that will start happening with Craig or if it only happens when people are dead.

The house is empty. I check the time. I walk into my room, but then I turn out the lights and go to Craig's room. A gloomy orange light comes in through the windows. I sit on the edge of his bed and look around. When Mom killed herself, I was out in the woods, oblivious to the fact that she was already dead. Craig could be dead somewhere, right now, and I wouldn't know.

I'm looking through the refrigerator when I hear the garage door opening and Dad's truck pulling in.

The refrigerator's light is out, but I can see well enough. There are three cans of beer, a gallon of milk that only has a swallow left, a Styrofoam carton of eggs, some American cheese slices, and a couple Tupperware containers that have been in there for weeks.

Dad walks in holding a case of Coors Light. I step away from the fridge, and he kneels in front of it, methodically taking the cans out one by one and placing them on the dark shelves. I take a plastic cup out of a cabinet and fill it full of water at the sink.

I got a call at work today from your school, he says.

I lean against the counter and take a drink.

Yeah? I say. Who called?

He looks at me and stops putting beer in the fridge.

I don't know, he says. What the hell does that matter?

He resumes his work of putting the beers away. The case is almost empty, and he has to sink his arm deep into the box, like he's putting it down into a hole. When he's finished, he rises with the last can in his hand and the empty box in the other. He kicks the door shut with his foot. He sets the box next to the garbage can and turns to look at me. He says nothing, just stares, and cracks open the can and takes a long drink.

After he swallows, he says, They said you disappeared from school at lunch.

I open my mouth to speak, but he beats me to it.

They said you've been getting into some trouble lately. Fighting and getting detention.

He drinks, and I wait for him to keep talking but he doesn't.

I'm having a bad week, Dad. That's all.

He stares.

I just needed to get out of there today.

He must see something in my face, hear something in my voice, because he only nods. If he'd gotten a call from school about Craig, he'd yell at him.

Did you take off with that girl of yours? They said you and some girl—Betty?—had ditched together.

Beth, I say.

Beth, he says. Don't matter. I ain't ready to be a grandfather, so you be careful what you do.

I stare at the floor.

Hear me?

Yes, I hear you.

He turns away toward the living room. He says, I thought maybe you'd gone the way of your brother.

I can feel heat rising to my face, and I want to shout at him for even mentioning Craig. But then he's gone from the room.

I cook myself a grilled cheese sandwich for dinner. When I'm done, I go to my bedroom and listen to tapes. I wait, hoping Beth will call, but she never does.

T he school bus is cold, with the seats like slabs of frozen stone. I sit by myself in the middle of the bus and lean against the metal sidewall, cold through my jacket and my sweatshirt underneath. The window is fogged, and I wipe the moisture away with the sleeve of my jean jacket. The sun is just coming up. The world only has hints of color.

I barely slept, thinking all night about Beth and Craig and Dad. I kept thinking about being dead. They say suicidal people always fantasize about what things will be like when they're gone. They picture their family members at the funeral. They picture kids at school talking about what happened, saying things like I shouldn't have picked on him or I wish I had talked to her more. You sort of imagine a future as if you're floating around as a ghost, getting to look at the world and how it responds. And they always say to tell suicidal people that this is a dangerous way to think because you won't be around to see it. You won't be around to see the mourning and the talking and to know how it affects your family.

I always wonder if my mom thought about this. If she thought about me, if she pictured me at the funeral, crying as Craig hugged me and Dad looked on, his eyes shell-shocked. She must have. She must have thought about the effect it would have on us. So when I think about this, when I see her seeing me, I realize just how bad it was for her. I don't see how she ever could have done it to me if she really saw me, really saw into the future and saw me holding Dad's gun, the same gun she used, putting it in my mouth. I don't see how she could have done it if she could imagine what it would do to me. So she must have been really bad off, worse than me. Whatever was wrong with her brain, it was worse than what's wrong with mine. And whenever I think about that, I forgive her because I know what kind of pain I'm in and if she was in worse pain than me I can't be mad that she wanted it all to end no matter how much it hurt me and Craig.

As the bus rides through the town and the blackness outside transforms to color, I think of myself floating around. I am dead.

I see Beth crying. I see her mom comforting her. I see Mr. James blaming himself. And Sergeant Frederickson coming to the house and seeing me as he saw my mother, telling himself he did everything he could. Doug and Luke and Dawn and Kenny, out at the junkyard, smoking, talking about how they wish they'd known me better. Gretchen, telling people she had thought Craig was the messed-up one. Jamie, maintaining a mask of indifference but inside happy that I'm gone—one brother down, one to go. Dad, sitting in front of the TV, drinking, wishing Craig was back so he could start anew with him. But Craig is gone, racing down the highway away from our town. He wouldn't even know I was gone.

That thought, that final thought, comforts me instead of saddens me. The thought of Craig, free, the Nova driving through highways flanked by cornfields or desert sagebrush. Let him be happy. Don't let him find out I killed myself.

I know this is all fantasy. I would not be a ghost, drifting in and out of the lives of the people I once knew. I would be gone, and there would be no way for me to perceive the world, no consciousness through which to see.

But in my daydream, as I lean against the window and stare out, I can't stop myself. In this dream, though, I see Mom. Like she's still alive. And I see her mourning. I see her at the funeral, not crying but with a sadness on her face worse than any I'd seen before. I see *her* finding *my* dead body.

I look around for Beth but she isn't among the students walking this way and that. I grab my book out of the locker, look around again, expecting to see her approach, and then I leave the freshman hall and walk down the sophomore hall. She isn't at her locker. I stand in the middle of all the people, who side step around me, and look around. I'm tall, so I can see over most of their heads. But I don't see her. As the people walk past, they all look at me, and I guess I'm not invisible like I used to be.

I walk to my first class, and my teacher says, It's nice of you to show up on time today.

In Algebra, Beth walks in just as the bell is ringing. The seats around me are already taken, and she has to sit across the room. She smiles at me and waves discreetly, and now I feel better.

Today she is wearing a KISS tee shirt, black with the name of the band in big red letters. Her jeans are ripped in several places, exposing the white of long underwear beneath.

She sees that I'm still looking at her, and she smiles and giggles and gives me a look that says she's flattered but that I'm going to have to turn and face the front of the class.

When the bell rings, I walk to Beth's desk and we exit together. She hugs me.

I have to talk to you, she says.

We stand in the hall because my next class is one way and hers is the other.

I'll tell you in lunch, she says. Meet me by the trophy case before you go into the cafeteria.

Tell me now, I say.

It's nothing, she says. I just want to tell you what happened with my mom.

I stare at the trophies, waiting for Beth. Behind the glass, gold-colored statues with placards are displayed for past championships in basketball, football, volleyball. There are team photographs, and in them the students are all trying to stand expressionless and tough. But behind the facade, each one of them is happy. Their expressions—tough, for the camera—betray the reality. They enjoy life. They are happy to be there, part of the team, part of the school. They're joyous in their youth, happy to be young.

My eyes shift, focus, and in the glass my own reflection is superimposed over the faces from past generations. My face, also expressionless, does not look like their faces. But I think maybe I'm becoming more and more like them. Good things seem to be happening for me. Even with Craig gone, I'm happier than I've been in a long time.

Out of the corner of my eye, in the reflection, I see Beth coming. She says, Hey. I turn and look at her, and I think that my expression must change and maybe now I look more like the people in the pictures. Just a little.

What did your mom say?

I'm grounded, she says. For two weeks. Which means I can't do anything this weekend. At all. She's such a bitch.

I'm sorry, I say.

You have nothing to be sorry for. It's my twat of a mother.

People walk around us, heading to the cafeteria.

Beth explains that she fought her mother, that she kept arguing that she was sick. But her mom threatened to tell the boyfriend about how she found her.

I'm not afraid of him, Beth says. It's just that he's a dick and he'd make all these snide comments about it. He'd call me a nudist. *Hey, why you got so many clothes on? If you want to walk around the house naked, I'm okay with it.* Ugh, I know exactly how he would act. I'd never hear the end of it.

We walk to the cafeteria, and Beth takes my hand.

Did your dad find out you skipped? she says.

Yeah, I don't think he cared.

You're lucky.

Beth is probably the lucky one. She has a mom who cares enough to ground her. But I don't say this out loud.

At lunch, Jamie Fergus sits on the other side of the cafeteria and never comes close to me. Moose Johnson sits at his side as he tells a story, animated, gesturing with his hands. Jamie is laughing and so are the rest of the people at the table.

What's yours, Danny?

I look around the table.

What? I say.

Everyone starts laughing: Dawn, Doug, Kenny, Luke. Beth doesn't laugh because she knows what I was thinking about as I was staring off.

We're talking about the greatest album of all time, Kenny says. Doug's is *Operation: Mindcrime*. Dawn's favorite, Kenny continues, is *Hysteria*, even though that's not even Def Leppard's best album.

Dawn flips him off and says, I changed mine anyway, dickhead. I switched to *Appetite for Destruction*, remember?

Oh yeah. He looks around. Luke's is *Number of the Beast*.

Great album, I say. What was yours?

Master of Puppets, Kenny says. Either that or Weird Al Yankovic.

Everyone laughs, except for Beth, who looks at me seriously.

What's yours? I say to her.

Back in Black, she says. Hands down.

Good choice.

You can't pick hers, Dawn says. Be your own man, Danny.

I think for a minute and then say, *Priest...Live.*

Fucking awesome album, Luke says.

Doesn't count, Kenny says. It's a live album. That's like picking a greatest hits album.

Oh, I say, well then I'll have to go with Weird Al.

When we're finished eating, we all carry our lunch trays to the garbage cans together. Jamie walks over there at the same time. He and Moose Johnson. Everyone is very quiet. I'm in line behind Beth and Kenny, and Jamie walks up next to me.

Hey, boy, he says. Your brother gonna skip the whole week?

I look at Jamie. I've had enough. I turn my tray and dump the garbage, and I let the tray fall into the can too. I want my hands to be free.

He says, Did your brother drop out because he knows—

I smack the bottom of his tray so it flips upward splattering ketchup and mustard and other colored gunk onto his blue sweater.

He looks at me with utter shock on his face, a drop of chocolate milk clinging to his cheek. I stand face to face with him, my heart pounding, and I say, Stay the fuck away from me.

Jamie is frozen in place but Moose Johnson steps forward so there's no way to escape. I'm surrounded, Moose and Jamie on one side, the line of garbage cans on the other. Mr. Delaney shoves through the aisles of tables trying to get to us, and Jamie still hasn't spoken because he doesn't know what to say. His face is burning like a red ember. His jaw muscles are pulsing.

He says, You're fucking dead.

Then Mr. Delaney is between us, putting a hand on each of our chests.

I saw that, Danny, he says. Go to the office.

I look at him and say, I don't know what you saw, but this clumsy son of a bitch almost spilled his whole tray on me.

Go to the office, Danny.

No.

I turn and walk away. There is a long, quiet pause, and I hear Mr. Delaney say to Jamie, Whatever you've got going on with that kid needs stop. This is getting out of control.

After my last period, I walk down the hallway to find all the contents of my locker scattered over the floor. My textbooks are torn in two at the spine. My notebooks are emptied. Paper fills the hall. My pictures in my locker—cutouts of bands and album covers from heavy metal magazines Craig used to buy—have been torn out and all that hangs on the door are tatters and pieces of tape.

I kneel down and slowly collect the torn-up books and pages, and start to pile them into the bottom of the locker. Stephanie, the girl who works in the office first period, kneels in her skirt and starts to help.

Thanks, Stephanie.

She smiles and doesn't say anything.

She is more careful than me, trying to match one half of the books with the other, placing them on the shelves instead of leaving them in a mound on the bottom, which is what I'm doing.

When we're done, I thank her again, and go to meet Beth at the back door of the school. The other students swarm the halls, joking, smiling. They head out to their cars or they walk over to their buses.

Beth says, My mom's dickhead boyfriend is coming to pick me up.

She walks over to the glass doors and looks out. He's sitting there, she says.

His truck is parked in the drop-off area in the way of everyone else coming and going.

Mom wants him to come by every day and pick me up so I don't go hanging out with bad influences.

You mean me?

She looks at me earnestly and says, I'm sorry, Danny.

It's not your fault, I say.

It's going to be okay, she says. This will all blow over in a week. Maybe then, if you asked nicely, we could go out on a real date.

I smile. Sounds good, I say.

Shit, she says. Here he comes. I've gotta go.

The boyfriend is walking up the sidewalk.

Beth gives me a hug, holds me tight, and then turns away to go. But it's too late, the boyfriend is coming through the doors and sees us.

Hey, he says to Beth, you know what your mom said.

Beth walks toward him. Yeah, she says, you're an unemployed loser who mooches off her.

I have my own business, he says.

Then why aren't you working?

Because I have to come pick your ass up from school so you stay out of trouble.

This is such bullshit, she says and walks past him.

He lingers for a minute, watching her go. Then he turns his head and stares at me. Other people go in and out of the doors but his eyes stay locked on me. He says nothing. Several seconds pass.

Beth calls to him. Take a picture, Jared. It lasts longer.

He walks after her. Beth gets to the truck first, tries the passenger door, and then stands waiting when she finds it's locked. Jared walks around the truck to the other side, gets in, starts the engine, and finally reaches over to lift the lock on her door.

The truck speeds away.

Most of the other students are gone now. The buses are loaded. The doors are starting to close on each one. I could walk out now and still catch mine, but I'm frozen in place. The first bus pulls away, then the second, and then mine starts to move and then it's gone.

I lean my forehead against the glass, cold on my skin. My breath fogs the surface. When there is a large cloud on the glass, I reach up and trace the outline of a pistol.

Danny, I hear a voice say.

I wipe the drawing off with the sleeve of my shirt and turn to see Mr. James.

Did you miss your bus? he says.

I'm waiting for a ride.

Do you have a minute? he says. I want to talk to you.

I say nothing and he adds, I know you don't want to talk. Just listen. I'll do the talking.

I sit on the bench next to the back door. The bench is metal like bleachers at a football field. I throw my legs out, lean back. He sits at the other end, on the edge, leaning forward, turned toward me. I put my hands in my pockets, lean the back of my head against the wall, and face forward.

Danny, he says, something's going on with you. I'm not sure what it is. I would guess it has something to do with your brother taking off. Maybe there's more.

He waits for a response and I say nothing.

Whatever it is, you're on a self-destructive path right now.

A student walks by and looks out the glass doors and sees she's missed the bus. She hurries back down the hall, looking as if she's about to cry.

I turn toward Mr. James. What's that supposed to mean? I say. I'm not *destroying* myself.

Yes you are, Danny. You're getting into fights. You're skipping school. You're making your own life more difficult.

I'm making my life difficult?

Yes. Listen to me. Really hear me.

I look at the floor. The carpet is old and orange, stained here and there with mud scuffs and spilled soda.

Mr. James says, I understand that you've had a rough life, Danny. You've experienced more hardship than anyone else your age should have to. You're not like these other kids.

He gestures with his hand, sweeping it in the direction of the hall as if it's filled with other students watching us.

They don't know what it's like to go through what you've gone through. They worry about grades and whether or not their parents are going to buy them cars. Whether or not someone will ask them to the dance. Whether they're going to win the next basketball game. You don't think about those things, do you, Danny?

I say nothing.

You are just trying to make it through the day.

He pauses and I wait.

You have to want to live. You have to *try*. But you also have to make decisions that help make your life better, not worse. If Jamie Fergus is starting shit with you, you can't get caught up in that. He has the luxury that he can be macho and tough and start fights. But what do you gain if you let him antagonize you? You're probably going to get your butt kicked. And if you do beat him up, you'll get kicked out of school. Maybe arrested. And if your brother steps in to help you, one of those things is going to happen to him.

What am I supposed to do? I say.

Walk away, he says. Be the bigger man and walk away. He might call you names or do something to antagonize you, but he won't flat-out *attack* you. Walking away might be harder for you to do than actually standing up and fighting, even against someone like Jamie Fergus, but that's just your male ego getting in the way. That's just this whole male machismo honor BS.

Do the hard thing, he says, and walk away. Don't let him coerce you into doing something stupid. He might call you a sissy and some people might think you're scared, but you should actually know that you've done the brave thing. You can't win if you fight him, even if you do win. I want you to think about the long term, Danny, because I don't think you really do. Fighting Jamie Fergus is a short-term problem, but you have a bigger, long-term goal.

What's that? I say, looking at him.

You want to live a happy life.

Doesn't everyone?

Yes, but some people don't have to try as hard as you. I'm sorry to say it, but that's the reality. You need to actually think about how to do it.

I look away from him, but now I'm thinking about what he's saying.

Mr. Bell and Mrs. Carver walk down the hall toward us, and when they see us talking, they turn and go the other way.

Your decisions now affect your future, Mr. James says.

A student walks by, and Mr. James and I are both quiet. It's Danielle, one of the girls who was there on Saturday night when Craig punched Jamie. She smiles at me and mouths the word *Hi*, and I nod back. She looks out the glass doors, sees her ride waiting, and walks outside. A blast of cold air hits us as the door slowly swings shut.

Mr. James says, Boys your age, Danny, don't usually think about the consequences of their actions. Things might not be going so good, and so you look for immediate relief. That's why people do drugs. That's why they get into trouble. You only think about the action, not the long-term effects. And then people get into trouble and make their lives even worse. But you've got to be smarter than that.

You're not lost yet, Danny. But if you're skipping school, getting into fights, doing whatever, it won't be long before you mess things up for yourself so badly that you won't be able to fix them. You, unlike a lot of these kids, have to *try* to make a better life for yourself. You can't just sit back and let a shitty life happen to you and then make excuses about why your life sucks.

You've been dealt a tough hand, he says, and life is hard. It's not fair that what comes so easy for some won't come easy for you, but that's just the way it is. So you have to be smart and make decisions that will make your life better in the long run, not worse.

He's quiet and I'm quiet. Down the hall we can hear muffled voices, but otherwise the school seems empty.

Does all that make sense, Danny?

I guess so, I say.

Mr. James's hand resting on the bench trembles a little. This makes me think about his words, knowing how important it was to him to deliver this speech and for me to understand it.

I understand, I say. Thanks.

Thanks for listening, he says.

I sit up straight. He rises.

You sure your ride's coming? he says.

Yeah, I say, they'll be here in a minute.

I rise and Mr. James offers his hand, and I shake it.

I say, I'm sorry I said what I said.

I appreciate that, he says.

He tells me to take care of myself and if I need help, I know where to find him. He turns down the hall. I wait for him to disappear around the corner. I look outside. The sky looks like dirty foam lathered across the atmosphere. Cold emanates from the glass. I put my palm against the glass and feel the chill against my skin. I push open the door and step out into the icy air to begin my long walk home.

I walk through the field coming out of town, and head toward the copse of trees where the backhoe sits with the mountains of dirt, both the dirt and the machine deposited there long ago for a construction project that never happened. I'm not paying attention. I'm looking around at the bruise-purple clouds, like tumors in a hemorrhaging brain, and I'm thinking about what Mr. James said. I feel good about it. Resolved to working on being happy, making things better for myself, not worse.

What he said makes sense in a way I never thought about before. I always assumed people were either happy or unhappy, not that they had much choice either way. I never thought about how you might need to actually work at being happy. And thinking about trying to be happy makes me realize, in a hopeful way, that I can succeed at this. Maybe I'll always be prone to sadness. But that doesn't mean I can't have a good life. That doesn't mean I can't enjoy certain parts—like yesterday with Beth—and focus on those parts and try to ignore the other stuff.

This is what I'm thinking about as I walk through the field. I'm feeling uplifted.

But then I see: parked in the clearing next to the backhoe is Jamie Fergus's Camaro. The exhaust pipe chugs out gray fumes, and now I hear the engine when I couldn't before. There are figures inside behind the glass. Several.

I stop.

I think about what Mr. James said. I consider turning around and going back the way I came. Or I could walk into the woods. But I move forward, into the clearing, walking toward the dirt road. I'm going to walk past, and I'm going to keep walking no matter what he says to me. He won't attack me, Mr. James said, not if I just walk away.

The driver's side door opens and Jamie steps out, looking over the hood at me. His varsity jacket is hanging open. He changed his lunch-splattered sweater. The passenger side opens and other guys from school step out. The first is Moose Johnson. From the backseat, two other guys climb out. I don't know their names but have seen them in the hall. Seniors. One wears an Ohio University sweatshirt with big green letters. He is taller than the others but thin, not big like Jamie or Moose, and his hair is spiked like Billy Idol's so he looks even taller. The other guy is shorter, with a ball cap and only a tee shirt even though it's cold. The shirt is a concert tee from the country band Alabama.

I keep walking and Jamie walks toward me. The others are staggered behind him. Jamie is smiling.

Well, well, well, Jamie says, like a character in a movie.

He has a beer in his hand and he knocks it back and tosses the empty into the dirt with a metallic ping.

I start walking again, but they fan out and block my path like four guard towers. I stop ten feet away.

Where do you think you're going? Jamie says.

Home, I say.

Why don't you hang out with us? We've got some beers. Want a beer?

I don't say anything.

What's the matter? he says. You don't like to drink?

The air is cold but my skin is hot underneath my sweatshirt. Inside my jacket pockets, I try to clench and unclench my fists, loosening my frozen fingers.

I hear your dad likes to drink, Jamie says. Is that why you don't drink? Because your dad's an alky?

I look from Jamie's face to the others. Moose looks bored, his chubby face—with a thick stubble like a thirty-year-old man—impassive and unreadable. The tall guy with spiked hair is smiling. The other guy, Alabama, looks off uncomfortably.

Did your dad start drinking before your mom killed herself? Jamie says. Or after?

I open my mouth to say something in response but stop myself. It will be harder *not* to fight, Mr. James said.

What about your brother? Jamie says. Was he always a pussy or did he just become one after your mom blew her brains out?

The four of them stand like posts in a fence, with three or four feet between each post. I think about walking forward, trying to go between them. But they'll close the gap and circle me.

I look at Jamie, and then I look away, thinking.

What did your mom—

He stops when I turn around and start walking in the direction I came from.

Hey, wait, he says. Where you going?

If I start running, they'll chase me. But if I'm able to walk out of the clearing and into the field behind, they might not follow. They might just let me go.

Hey, come back here, peckerwood.

The sound of footsteps in the dirt.

I'm talking to you, you fucking faggot.

Jamie is next to me now, looking at me as he keeps up. The others are a few paces behind.

Beyond the clearing, the field stretches, empty. The buildings from town look a long way away. I pull my hands out of my pockets.

Hey, Jamie says, grabbing my arm. Stop fucking walking.

I spin and yank my arm out of his grasp. We're face to face. I stare at him. He spits in my face. I feel his hot breath. The spittle is warm at first then turns cold.

How do you like it, bitch?

I try to wipe the spit away with my arm. The others circle around me.

Leave it, he says.

I ignore him and try to wipe the rest. He grabs my arm again, and I shove him back, hard, so he has to take a few steps backward to keep from falling down.

And then it begins.

Moose Johnson grabs me from behind. I try to pull away, but he is strong, and Jamie is back in front of me, swinging his big fist into my body. Each blow is like a depth charge, exploding waves of pain through my body. I try to hunch over to give Jamie a smaller target, but Moose has my arms and is pulling me back. Jamie hits me again in the ribs and I forget how to breathe.

I swing my head backward, and the back of my skull connects with Moose's mouth and his grip loosens, for just an instant, and I squirm and twist and I'm free, backpedaling away from the group.

Fuck, Moose says in a deep baritone voice. That motherfucker is dead.

He grits his teeth, which are slick with saliva and blood. Jamie rushes past him, coming at me, and I turn and run. I head toward the backhoe, remembering the games Craig and I played when I was a kid and how I used the high ground of the machine to defend myself from make-believe hoards.

I get one hand on the metal to pull myself up, but Jamie grabs my jacket. I throw my elbow at his face and connect solidly with his nose, hard enough to knock him back onto his butt in the dirt. But the tall kid grabs me by the jacket and pulls and I stumble backward as he propels me into the dirt. I'm up off the ground in an instant, but the kid with the Alabama shirt is there, not attacking but just cutting off my path of escape.

I can't think, can't keep up with all that's happening, and as I'm looking around, trying to figure out what to do, Moose Johnson comes at me, fast for how big he is, and he tackles me like I'm a quarterback frozen in the pocket. He lifts me off the ground and drives me down into the dirt with his shoulder. My breath leaves me and I feel like he must have broken something inside of me because I can't pull any air back in. I try to move and squirm, but I can't. He drives his fists into my body, each one paralyzing me to stop the next.

Let me at him, Jamie says.

Moose hits me one more time and then rises up. They're all standing around me, like surgeons looking down at a patient. Jamie's nose is bleeding. He wipes some onto his fingers and holds his hand down to me.

You see this, you little fucker?

He squats down, grabs my jacket with one hand and raises his fist with the other, but then I grab him and wrap him up and we're rolling in the dirt. My hands are on his throat, and I am on top of him, and his face is turning red, and I raise a fist to smash it into his nose again, but someone kicks me in the ribs and someone else grabs me by the hair and pulls me off, and then Jamie is on top of me. He hits me once in the face and everything goes black for a moment. Then I'm hardly aware that he's hitting me in the body. I don't feel any of the punches. They seem far away. When they stop and Jamie rises, then I feel the pain, coming back, like the nerves carrying the hurt were delayed somehow.

I roll onto my side, like a fetus, holding my stomach. My face is in the dirt, and I look at the ground and somehow every grain of dust, every rock, seems to be in focus and yet none of the rest of the world is.

Jamie starts to kick me and so does the tall kid. I squirm and move and try to shield myself with my arms, but there are two of them and I can't move fast enough.

The kid in the Alabama shirt says, I think that's enough, Jamie.

Fuck that, Jamie says.

I'm serious, man.

Jamie bends over and drives his fist into my face and that stops everything. It's like I'm asleep but I'm awake. I can see the world but everything is coming through a filter and I can't understand what's going on, what's being said. I should move, but everything I do is slow. I roll onto my stomach and begin to crawl.

Jamie and Alabama are arguing.

If your dad finds out, Alabama says, he'll—

Shut the fuck up about my dad!

A fist grabs hold of my hair and Jamie drags me on my butt. I grab his hands and hold on and turn and try to get up, but I can't get my footing, and he tosses me in the dirt next to his Camaro. I lie there on my side. The others walk toward us. Jamie is getting something out of his car. He comes back with a tire iron, holding it from the sharp, pointed end.

Alabama says, What the hell are you doing, man?

Jamie gets in his face, and the two argue. I should get up. I should run. But I can't even stand.

You're gonna kill him, Alabama says.

So what, Jamie says.

He turns and raises the metal bar. I don't recoil from it or try to move. I just look at it, raised in the air, with the gray clouds behind. And then it comes down, but instead of hitting me in the head, Jamie smashes it into my leg between my knee and hip. I gasp and reach for the pain as if I can muffle it because this hurts worse than anything they've done so far. He raises the iron again. I close my eyes.

I wish he will hit me in the head so I can die.

But the next blow doesn't come. There's more arguing. Alabama and Jamie are shouting at each other. I can't make out the words they're saying. Jamie drops the tire iron in the dirt. It's only a foot or two away, but it might as well be at the edge of the solar system because I would never be able to get to it.

It must be over, I think, and then I hear the sound of a zipper and I know it's a zipper for jeans and I know what's coming.

You're an asshole, Jamie, Alabama says.

A jet of liquid sprays onto my back and my head, in my hair, in my ear. The urine is warm and stinks. I put my hands over my head, and then another one of them—Moose probably—starts to piss on me too. On my jacket. On my jeans.

You guys are fucking sick, Alabama says.

They zip up. My eyes are closed and I'm curled in a ball, my arms around my head. But I can hear the metallic sound of Jamie picking the tire iron up out of the dirt. I can't see him, but I know he kneels down next to my back. He nudges me with the iron.

Now, Danny, he says calmly, his voice nasally because of the bloody nose, if you tell anyone about this, do you know what I'm going to do?

I lie quietly.

I'm gonna rape that little girl you've been hanging out with.

He laughs and spits on me again. I lie on my back and look up at him. I don't wipe away the spit.

He stares at me, and I will myself not to cry.

Finally, he looks away. The four of them climb into the car, and Jamie spins the tires in the dirt as he drives away. The car disappears in a cloud of dust. And then I see it, small, cruising along the highway with the other cars like none of this happened.

My face throbs. Sharp lightning bolts of pain strike my leg, my chest, my arms. It hurts to breathe, so I take short, shallow breaths that won't inflate my lungs. I smell of sour urine. I sit up but dizziness comes over me. I lean over and puke, a foamy pile that steams in the cold. I heave again but nothing comes out. Every retch feels like it's breaking my ribs and so I clench my teeth and stop myself from heaving again. I lie on my side, face in the dirt. I stare at the backhoe. I think of when Craig and I used to play on it and I want to cry, so I roll over and look the other way.

I don't know how long I lie there. My body shivers in the cold, but I don't get up. I'm not asleep but I'm not awake. The field is sideways. I see a bird fly across my vision. A rabbit hops from one clump of vegetation to another. I stop shivering and don't feel cold anymore. I close my eyes to sleep but I think about my father coming home from work, and it suddenly feels important to get to the house before he does.

I sit up. I crawl to my hands and knees. I rise and stand. I take a deep breath of the cold air and wince and bend over, holding myself as if that will stop the pain. I take a step. Then another. And then I'm walking.

The walk is a blur that, at once, seems to take hours and then is over before I expect. When I open the front door, I can't seem to understand how I got there. The phone is ringing and I let it. When the answering machine picks up, the caller leaves no message. I go to the bathroom and look at myself in the mirror. The left side of my face is red, turning purple, but it's not as bad as it feels. I expected to look like the Elephant Man, my face swollen to the point of deformity. Clumps of wet hair are tangled and crisp, frozen from the cold. And there are a few streaks of dirt on my face. My jacket and jeans are dirty too, but that's it. I could pass for having spent an afternoon hiking. There's no blood, no open wounds.

I pull my jacket off. My shirt. My jeans. Now I see the damage. Red marks, bruises, lumps of swollen skin. I almost start to cry but stop myself again.

I step into the shower, the porcelain cold on my feet. The phone starts ringing again, but when I turn the water on I can't hear it. I adjust the temperature so the water is as hot as I can take, and I stand under it, turning, letting the heat run over me. I don't soap. I don't scrub. I sit down on the floor and let the water hit me and I try not to think. The water begins to cool and I turn it off. I sit for several minutes but then I start to shiver so I will myself to stand and dry off.

I carry my clothes to my room and take the towel from around my waist and put on sweatpants and a sweatshirt. It seems as if my actions are done by someone else. I move slowly, walk slowly. I'm sitting on the bed, putting on a pair of socks when the phone rings again. I let it. The answering machine picks up and there's silence.

I start to lie down, and the phone rings again.

Jesus Christ, I say, and I stand and walk down the hall.

Hello.

Hey, Danny!

It's Craig's voice. Relief goes through me, and I can feel a physical change, like just the sound of his voice is enough to start the healing process.

Hey, I say, and I want to say more but I don't know what to say.

I pick up the base of the phone and carry it over to the couch, stretching the cord across the floor.

Where the hell have you been? he says. I've been trying to catch you before Dad gets home.

Sorry, I say.

How the hell are you, bro?

I'm okay, I say.

My voice cracks a little and I feel like I'm going to cry, and I hope that Craig can't hear the change in my voice.

Where are you? I say.

Far away, man. Far away.

He asks me what has happened since he left, and I'm silent because all I can think about is Jamie and his friends in the clearing by the backhoe. He asks what Dad said when he realized he was gone. I don't know what to say to this, so I tell him about how the police showed up asking about him.

He laughs, and I'm waiting for him to tell me that he stole the money but he doesn't say and I don't ask.

I want to tell him I miss him but I don't because I don't want him to come back. I want him to stay gone, free from the life here. I want to picture him driving away, through fields and by lakes and into mountains, exploring the world and starting over.

Have you seen that bitch Gretchen? he says.

She came by the locker to talk to me, I say.

Did she thank you for saving her life?

No, I say.

What'd she say?

She told me that I should stay away from Jamie Fergus because he's been giving me a hard time since you left.

He has?

I don't say anything. I want the conversation to change, but part of me doesn't want it to. I want to tell someone what's been happening, but I shouldn't tell Craig because I don't want him to worry about what happens back here. I want him to stay gone and live a new life.

Danny, tell me what Jamie Fergus did.

I can't help it anymore. I start crying, and through a whiny, choked voice I tell him that he's been saying he's gonna kick Craig's ass and that he started a fight with me at school and I would have just walked away but he said something about Mom and I couldn't help myself. I tell him about what happened after school today, but it comes out in sobs and blabbering, and I don't know how he understands any of it. I tell him they spit on me and hit me with a tire iron, but I don't mention that they pissed on me.

He's quiet, and I sniff and wipe my nose with my shirtsleeve.

Danny, he says, I want you to tell me who the other people were.

One was Moose Johnson, I say. I don't know the other guys. One was real tall. The other guy wasn't. He wore an Alabama tee shirt.

I know who they are, he says. Stan Gabbard and Darren Christensen.

The guy in the Alabama shirt tried to stop 'em, I say. But he couldn't.

I bet he didn't try very hard, Craig says.

I don't say anything.

Okay, Danny, I don't want you to worry about anything. I'm coming back.

No, Craig. Please.

I'm coming back, he says. I'm gonna take care of those motherfuckers.

I plead and tell him that he shouldn't worry about me. That I'm fine.

Don't do anything, Craig.

You just steer clear of them until I get back, he says. Those motherfuckers are dead.

When he hangs up, I sit on the edge of the couch thinking. I felt relieved when I was telling him, but now I feel guilty. I see his car driving back, and I wish it was driving away. I'm a child. A baby. I hate myself for crying and for telling him the things I did.

I wish I could call him and talk him out of it, but I don't know where he is.

I go into my room and turn out the lights. I pull the blanket and sheet back, and I lie down and pull them up to my neck and try to keep them snug around me. I lie with my eyes open and stare at the ceiling as the light from the window fades and the room goes dark. I hear Dad come home. He doesn't come to see if I'm in my room, and I don't get up to say anything to him.

Every breath hurts my ribs. My body aches. Every once in a while a chill will run through my body, like I'm fighting off a virus. I still smell urine, faintly, and I don't know if it's my jacket and jeans lying in the corner or if the smell is in my mind.

I don't turn on any music, and it's a long, long time before I fall asleep.

D ad opens my door. It must be late at night and he's checking on me before he goes to bed.

I'm going to work, he says. Don't you dare miss school after the shit you pulled earlier this week.

Okay, I say.

I feel like I'm far away and we're talking through water. I wonder why he's going back to work at night.

Where the hell were you last night? he says.

Then it hits me: it's morning.

Right here, I say, my voice thick and rough. I didn't feel well.

It's still dark enough in the room that he can't see my face.

He doesn't say anything for a few seconds, and then says, Well, I ain't calling the school and telling 'em you're sick. You already got one day off this week.

He turns away, leaving the door open. I hear him down the hall: his boots on the floor, the jingle of his keys. Then the house is quiet. I sit up. My mouth is dry, tongue like sandpaper. I stand and it feels like weights are strapped to me. Each bruise is like an injection of metal in my skin, inorganic and resistant to every move.

It takes effort to get dressed. I concentrate on my movements, moving the clothes gently over the bruises, controlling my breathing. When I'm finished, I look through the clothes I wore yesterday to get the two hundred dollars out of the pocket of my jean jacket. I can't see where the urine is so I try to touch as little of the jacket as I can.

I'm hungry and feel like I've lost ten pounds. I make myself scrambled eggs. But I only eat a few bites before I start to feel sick.

I find a bottle of Advil in the medicine cabinet and count out four pills. I turn on the faucet and lean down and cup my hands and drink. The pills feel thick as they slide down my throat, like my neck is swollen inside.

I try to comb my hair in the bathroom mirror, but it's matted and tangled from sleep, and so I let it stay shaggy.

In the closet is Dad's big military coat, a dull green color, like the one the guy wears in *Taxi Driver*, and I pull it out and put it on. It has big inside pockets, and I go to the gun cabinet and look inside.

The Magnum is there. Kneeling, I look at it for a long time but don't pick it up. I reach past it to Dad's hunting knife. I pull it out of its sheath. The blade is at least six inches long, curving slightly at the tip, and the handle is metal but colored in a way that looks like wood. The knife is somehow heavy and light at the same time. Craig and I used to call it Dad's Rambo knife, but it's not the same. It's for skinning deer. The metal has tarnished over time, but it's sharp enough to cut through the breastplate and to split the pelvis so the deer is open from its asshole to its throat, and it's easy to dump all its guts out onto the ground and let the blood drain.

I sheathe the knife and put it in the coat's big inside pocket, and then I stand in front of the mirror and look to make sure no one will be able to see the outline of it. I think for a few seconds, and I put the knife back. I walk out to the garage and look around. There is a five-gallon bucket filled with pipe of various lengths and sizes, scrap Dad brought home from work for whatever reason. I take a piece that hasn't been bored out: a solid piece of steel about a foot long. I put it in the vice and take a hacksaw and cut all but a few inches. The remaining piece fits inside my fist—like a roll of quarters, but heavier.

I slip it into my coat pocket and practice reaching for it. I hear the bus, its loud familiar sound, and I walk quickly—the fastest I've moved all morning—to the door and step outside into the cold. I climb up into the bus, and each step is agony. I collapse into a cold seat and look out the window. A light snow has begun to fall.

After I go to my locker, I leave Dad's green coat on.

Beth comes toward me down the hall. Today she's wearing a skirt and a red blouse, and she seems almost dressed up like a preppy girl. She's smiling. Then she sees my face and says, Jesus Christ, what happened?

Nothing, I say.

Danny, please tell me what happened.

Nothing happened, Beth.

I turn and walk away.

— *120*

Danny, she says.

But I keep walking, and she lets me go. As I turn the corner, Gretchen is coming toward me.

Hey, I'm looking for you, she says.

So.

Where's your brother?

None of your fucking business.

I turn to walk away, and she grabs my arm. She looks for the first time—really looks at me—and says, Holy shit, what happened to your face?

Don't pretend you don't know.

Jamie said he and the guys were horsing around playing football, she says. He said that's how he got a bloody nose.

She's still holding my arm and I jerk it away.

Look, Danny, all I know is that your brother called me yesterday saying he was gonna kill Jamie and Jamie is a dead man. Shit like that. I just want all this to stop before somebody really gets hurt.

I stare at her. Her skin is flush and there's something about the look on her face that shows real fear. Even when Craig was walking toward her with a gun, she didn't look like this.

People are walking all around us in the hallway, hurrying because the bell is about to ring.

I lean toward Gretchen, staring at her, and say, You want this to stop before somebody gets hurt? They took a tire iron to me, Gretchen. I think that time has already passed.

And then I turn and walk away.

The bell rings when I'm five seconds from the door of my first class. I walk in, and when Mrs. Carver sees me she opens her mouth and lifts her arm to point toward the office, but then she looks me in the face and drops her arm and doesn't say anything.

In Algebra, Beth sits next to me. She looks at me with concern, but I don't acknowledge that I see it.

The teacher is writing math problems on the board. My math book is open and my notebook is out, but I'm staring forward like I'm in a trance. I don't hear what she's saying. It still hurts to breathe. My body aches. I can feel the swollen skin on my face, pulsing like a tumor. My mind keeps experiencing flashes of what happened: Jamie pulling me by the hair, Moose tackling me, my face in the dirt. Crying to Craig. I want to stop the memories, but I can't.

Beth passes me a note. I open it and it says,

You can tell me.

I fold the note and put it in my textbook. I close the book and slide it to the corner of my desk.

Beth passes me another note. I put this one inside the textbook without opening it. She doesn't try again. She faces forward, pretending to pay attention. When class ends, she takes her book and notepad into her arms and walks out of the classroom without looking at me.

At lunchtime, I wait in the restroom until I think the line has died down. Beth is sitting with Dawn and Doug and Luke and Kenny. I don't look at them directly. Jamie Fergus is standing over a table of friends, laughing. When I buy my lunch, I turn to leave the cafeteria. Mr. Delaney stops me and asks what I'm doing leaving the lunchroom with my tray. I tell him that Mr. James wanted me to go eat lunch with him in his office. He looks at me, looking at the new bruises on my face, thinking about what I said and how it could almost make sense, and then he lets me go.

I walk to the other side of the school, trying my best not to limp too noticeably. When I pass students, I act as if carrying my lunch tray through the hall is normal. In the hallway near Mr. James' office, I step into the bathroom and set my tray on the sink. I sit on the counter and lean against the mirror. I'm eating when another student walks in, a junior who is no one special. He stops when he sees me, and he looks at me for a second, and then he turns around and walks out.

My appetite is voracious, but I can only eat about half of the food before I feel sick. It hurts to swallow and chew, and down inside me it feels like things are broken internally and normal functions like breathing and digestion don't work right anymore.

When I'm finished, I sit and think and hurt.

I dump the lunch, tray and all, into the garbage. I stand in front of the urinal, but only a little bit of bright yellow piss comes out, hot like acid.

I walk back to the cafeteria and look. Beth is gone. Jamie Fergus is still there. I walk to the table where Beth was sitting without turning in the direction of Jamie Fergus's table.

Hey man, Kenny says, where were you today?

What happened to your face? Luke asks me.

Got up to take a leak last night and I ran into the doorjamb in the dark.

Kenny giggles like this is funny.

Ouch, says Doug.

I'm still standing, and I say, Hey, could one of you give me a ride to Wal-Mart after school? There's something I need to pick up.

Doug says he can do it. I linger for another couple minutes, talking, and then I turn to go. Out of the corner of my eye, I can see Jamie sitting at his table, but I don't turn to look at him.

After school, the guys are waiting for me in the parking lot. I don't want to hang out, but I need the ride. The roads are slushy, and the fields and yards are coated in a thin sheen of white. My ribs and muscles ache. I lean my head against the window of Doug's car and look out and think about how rude I was to Beth today.

Inside Wal-Mart, we walk to the music section where we start to browse the tapes. Everyone is talking about good albums to buy.

I tell the others I'll be right back, and before they ask where I'm going, I leave the section and walk through the store to sporting goods. An employee is behind the counter, a guy who can't be much older than Craig.

He asks if he can help me, and I say I'm just looking. I wander around as if I don't know what I'm looking for, but I know right where the ammunition is. When I walk to that shelf, scanning for the box I'm looking for, the clerk says, You have to be eighteen to buy ammunition.

I walk past to hunter-orange vests and camouflage coats. I wait and wait, and I think I'm not going to be able to do it. Finally, another customer walks into the section.

Hey, Dale, the clerk says to him.

How's it hanging, Jerry?

They start talking, standing on opposite sides of a display case full of knives. I walk back to the ammunition. I pick up a box of shells, hold it on the other side of my body, and disappear behind a shelf. There's a mirror in the corner, a big round one that lets him see throughout the section, but I turn my back to it and stuff the box inside Dad's green coat. I put my hands in the pockets on the outside because people might be able to see the outline otherwise.

I don't look in the direction of the clerk as I'm leaving the sporting goods area. I walk toward the music section where the others are and chance a glance over my shoulder. The clerk is following me. I duck into a toy aisle and walk past the rows of *Star Wars* and G.I. Joe figures. I pull the ammunition out and hide it behind a box for He-Man's Castle Grayskull. I walk to the end of the aisle and then, from the opposite end, the clerk says, Hey!

I wait as he approaches.

I saw you steal that ammo, he says.

What ammo?

Don't play stupid with me, kid.

He has pimples across his forehead like he's been shot over and over by a BB gun.

Empty your pockets, he says.

I reach into one of my coat pockets and pull out a wad of the money Craig gave me. Not all of it, but enough that his eyes widen. I reach in the other and pull out the fist-sized piece of pipe.

Where's the ammo, kid?

I hold the fistful of money out toward him.

He frowns.

I gesture for him to take it.

Is that a bribe? he says.

Take this and leave me alone, I say.

He stares at me, and we're both quiet. He looks behind him and then glances in the direction behind me. He snatches the money. One of the bills drops and he leans down to pick it up. When he stands, he starts to backpedal slowly.

You're lucky, he says.

You're lucky I don't beat your fucking brains in, I say.

His eyes squint and he freezes, looking at me carefully to see if I mean what I say. Then he turns and hurries out of the aisle.

I pull what's left of my money out and count it. I gave the guy eighty bucks.

I kneel and move the Castle Grayskull out of the way. I put the box of shells back into my coat.

When I return, Luke says, Where've you been, dude?

Sorry, I say. I had to take a piss.

What did you want to come here for? Kenny asks.

I wanted to get a tape, I say.

I look quickly through the cassettes then pull out a Megadeth album. This one, I say.

Awesome, says Kenny. I saw one of their videos the other day on *Headbangers Ball*.

You guys gonna get anything?

They all say they have no money, and we go to the registers. I keep my one hand in my pocket, hiding the box of bullets.

When we walk outside and pile into Doug's car, he says, Let's listen to that tape, Danny.

I hand it forward, and Luke takes a few minutes getting it out of the package while Doug drives. He puts it into the player. We all sit and listen.

Is this about nuclear war? Doug says.

Luke says yes and the others start talking about how the Russians have enough missiles to blow up the world twenty times, but we have enough to blow it up thirty. They start talking about whether they think a war like that will ever really happen.

They don't know that I have a box of nuclear missiles in my pocket.

They ask if I want to hang out, but I tell them that I need to get home. Doug offers to give me a ride to school in the morning.

When they drop me off, I still have a few hours before Dad gets home.

I take the Magnum out of the gun cabinet. The shells are in one inside pocket, and I place the gun in the other. Both weigh the coat down, and it's easy to see from the outside that there's something inside. But they do fit and you can't tell what they are.

I take a paper bag from under the sink and pick through the garbage, pulling out cans. I pull the ones on the top. When I have to go deeper into the trash to cans covered in coffee grinds and eggshells, I quit.

I step out the back door and walk through the yard and into the field behind the house. The frozen dirt in the field is frosted with white. It hurts more to breathe in the cold. The place where they hit me in the face throbs, like it's made of some other kind of meat and responds differently to the cold air.

At the back of the field, I come to a barbed-wire fence—rusted from weather and time—that forms the barrier to a copse of woods. I climb over, and the effort it takes is surprising. My legs feel heavy. Every branch is leafless. The trees look dead. How weird it is that they can survive a winter and be reborn anew each spring.

I find the spot I usually go to. A clearing at the end of a dirt path, with an old disused fire pit and the bench seat from an old pickup torn out and sitting like a couch. A log that's almost flat lies on one side of the clearing, and I start setting the beer cans up there. Every movement is a labor.

I upright two logs, sawed-off stumps about two feet tall, and brush them off, then sit on one. I pull out the box of shells, open it, and set it on the other log. Cold wetness comes in through my jeans from the stump. I pull out the gun—it's ice cold—and open the chamber. I plug bullets into the slots one at a time. I close the gun and I hold it in my hand, thinking about what it's done and what it could do.

I stand back about twenty paces from the cans. My feet are wet through my tennis shoes, and my toes are starting to burn from the cold.

I lift the gun, line up the sight, take my time, control my breathing.

The bullet explodes from the barrel, lifting the gun with the recoil.

The first can makes a clanking noise as it bounces backward into the woods.

I shoot the second can, then the third, and on down the line until the gun is empty and I've hit every can I aimed at.

I stand with the gun at my side, breathing heavily. I don't notice the pain in my ribs now. My face is no longer throbbing. I walk back to the stumps through the wet leaves and glazing of snow. My ears are ringing.

I load the gun again. The chamber is hot, but my fingers are cold and can hardly tell the difference between the two temperatures. Both burn.

This time I stand only about ten paces from the three cans that are left. I hold the gun at my side, dangling, uncocked. I bring the gun up fast, cocking it in the motion, and point and aim and squeeze all as fast as I can. I blast the can into the woods, move my arm to the side, shoot the next, and then the next. Hitting them all in a matter of seconds.

I load the three empty chambers. I look around the fire pit and find a couple beer bottles. I stuff my fingers in the mouth holes to carry them in one hand. I don't set down the gun. I put the bottles where I had put the cans, and I walk across the clearing all the way to the other side. Any farther and I would be in the trees. The bottles must be fifty yards away. I hold the gun up with both hands, close my left eye. The sight is nearly as big as the bottle itself. My hand wavers. The target is so small that the sight veers from it with every movement. I steady myself. I think of the bottle as Jamie's face. I begin to squeeze. The gun goes off and the bottle shatters. The bottles were too close together, and the exploding glass knocks the other one onto the ground in front of the log. I shoot it where it lays.

I put the gun away and pick up the box of shells. When I step out of the woods, snow is starting to fall again in fat gray flakes, like ash coming down from a nuclear winter.

Back inside, I feel tired, weak, like I haven't eaten or slept and I've just been going on nerves and adrenaline. I go to my room and look through my cassettes, but I can't find anything I want to listen to so I lie down in the bed and pull the covers over me and sit in silence. I wait for my body heat to fill the cocoon of blankets and warm me up. I'm too exhausted and numb to do anything but think.

When Dad comes home, he opens my bedroom door. The room is dark. The only light comes from the hallway and a blue glow from the edge of the window blinds.

You alive? he says.

Unfortunately.

Don't you fucking talk like that, Danny.

I'm alive, I say.

He waits and I don't get out of bed or say anything.

You go to school today? he asks.

Yeah.

You okay? You really sick?

I'll be all right.

He waits again, and there's silence. The blankets are wrapped around me, but still I feel cold.

Any word from your brother? Dad says.

I don't say anything.

I'm worried about him, Danny.

I haven't heard from him, I say softly, my voice on the verge of cracking.

He never was worth a damn anyway, Dad says.

I thought you were worried about him, I mutter

My father closes the door. I don't know whether he heard me or not.

I listen as Dad watches *Cheers*. I recognize the music and hear Sam's voice, and then I'm asleep.

I wake up sometime in the night and can't fall back asleep. I lie, eyes open in the darkness, for thirty minutes or an hour, and then I rise. I put on Dad's coat in the dark. I walk down the hall to the living room. Dad is on the couch—asleep or passed out, it's the same with him—still wearing his work clothes. My eyes have adjusted and the light in the living room is gray.

I open the bottom compartment of the gun cabinet. I open the box of shells. One by one, I plug the bullets into the gun. I walk back toward my room. I stop. I turn. I look at Dad.

I raise the gun.

At this angle, the bullet would break through his teeth, hit the roof of his mouth, and explode out the back of his skull, disappearing into the couch and bringing with it blood and skull and memories. I imagine the quick jerk of his body as an eruption of gelatinous brain soaks the couch. I imagine the cloud of smoke in the air and blood bubbling up out of his mouth, red foam oxygenated from the last nervy exhalation of his lungs. His eyes drifting open and staring vacantly at me the way hers did.

It's your fault he left, I say aloud to my father. It's your fault she's dead.

He continues sleeping. I thumb the hammer back.

I should do it, I say. But she wouldn't want me....

By *she*, I'm not sure which one I mean. Mom or Beth.

I lower the Magnum.

I place my thumb on the hammer, and my father continues to sleep through the quiet click as I uncock the gun.

Up on the roof, I sit and shiver in the cold. The metal is cold in my hand. I place the cold barrel under my chin. I put it against my head. The gun is loaded this time, and it's heavier.

I cock it. I put it in my mouth. It wouldn't take much weight from the finger to set it off, but I touch the trigger anyway. The barrel is like an ice cube in my mouth. My lips stick to the steel. My breathing is heavy, and my ribs hurt with each movement of my lungs. My exhalations come out white on each side of the gun. I look at the sky. I think of the magnitude of the universe. I don't matter. I don't matter. I think of Beth, and I think of Craig, and I think of my mother. And I think my last thought should be of her. But I can't think of her without thinking of the way she looked with the hole through her head, the afternoon sun coming in the window and hitting the blood. The brightness of the blood. I close my eyes and try to remember her another way but I can't. I'm sorry, Mom. I'm sorry. I'm sorry. I'm sorry.

I pull the gun out and uncock it and sit and wipe the tears from the corners of my eyes. I cry, and I hug my legs to my chest and keep crying. And I hate myself for crying. I hate myself because I couldn't do it. And because I even wanted to. If I don't go through with it, if I live through the next week or next year or next however long, I will always hate myself. I will never know how to not hate myself.

D ad has left for work. I'm sitting on the edge of my bed. I'm dressed. I'm waiting for Doug to come pick me up. I'm holding the Magnum and staring at it. I'm thinking about taking it to school, imagining all of the scenarios.

I'm imagining Jamie coming up to me at lunch, dumping my tray in my lap or saying something about my mother. I stand. I pull the gun out of my coat. I level it at his chest. As he opens his mouth to protest, I pull the trigger and knock him backward. He is sucking in his last breaths, coughing out blood. The lunchroom is screaming. I line up the sight between his eyes. My finger is on the trigger. The hair trigger. The gun goes off.

And then what happens?

I go to prison for the rest of my life. Or I get gunned down in a faceoff with police. I turn the Magnum on myself.

Or another possibility. I pull the gun but don't use it. And then I go to juvenile hall.

But I don't think that latter option would happen. If I pull the gun, I will end up using it. Jamie might act like he isn't scared. He might say something like, You ain't got the balls, kid. I would do it. I would squeeze the trigger and surprise him and surprise everyone.

I stare at the gun. The stainless steel reflects my own blurry image, my features warped and twisted with the curves of the gun. The gun is four pounds, empty, but it feels like fourteen. Now it's loaded with six bullets, and it feels heavier still. But it feels light too, when I think about what it can do. How can something so small do so much?

In the metal, my warped reflection stares back at me. I move the gun closer to my face, and the blurred image changes, my jaw becoming elongated, my eyes widening and hollowed like the sockets in a skull.

A car horn beeps outside.

I stare at the gun for a few more seconds, unmoving, thinking. I rise, turn, lift the mattress of the bed with one hand. I hide the gun inside the bed. I'll be home before Dad, so it doesn't really matter, but I hide it anyway.

I walk outside into the cold, and Doug is there waiting with Kenny and Luke in the car with him. The exhaust pipe chugs out white fumes. The sky is clear and the sun, just rising, seems to give the air a heavenly glow.

Beth isn't at her locker, so I go looking for her. I thought the pain would be lessened today but it isn't. It's only different. An ache now, throughout my body, even the parts they didn't hit.

Eight minutes till the bell rings. I walk through the halls purposefully, first the sophomore hallway and then the junior and finally the senior. There she is: talking to Dawn and Gina and a girl I've never met but whose name I think is Hailey.

Well, look what the cat dragged in, Dawn says.

Can I talk to you? I say to Beth.

Go ahead, she says.

She flips her hair back, and I can tell she's upset with me. She's wearing a Dokken tee shirt and her jean jacket, hanging open. She wears dark makeup around her eyes, and the color of her irises jumps out. I feel sick inside, seeing her.

Alone? I say.

She thinks about it, and before she makes a decision, Dawn laughs and says, We'll leave you two lovebirds so you can kiss and make up.

Beth gives her the finger.

When we're by ourselves, I look at her and say, I'm sorry.

For what? she says defiantly.

I was an asshole.

Her face changes. I see the hardness breaking apart.

I walk into class just as the bell rings.

Just in the nick of time, huh, Danny?

I smile at the teacher, and she smiles back.

Five minutes haven't gone by when the voice of Mr. Kerr comes over the PA system, announcing my name and telling me to come to the office. Normally they say please at the end, but Mr. Kerr doesn't.

In the office, Stephanie says hi and smiles.

How are you? I say.

Before she can answer, Mr. Kerr steps out of his office and beckons me in to see him.

I sit and he sits across from me.

We're moving your lunch period, he says.

I say nothing.

You're going to have C lunch from now on. Do I need to tell you why?

Why me and not him?

Your schedule is easier to change around, that's all. We're going to move one of your study halls to before lunch instead of after.

He sits back in his chair, looks out the window to the street. The sun is coming in, mixing with the beige walls and giving the room a urine-yellow glow.

He leans forward to pick up a pen. He plays with it, passing it back and forth between his hands.

Listen, he says, I don't want to see you anywhere near Jamie Fergus. And don't worry: we've had this conversation with him. You two need to steer clear of one another.

I say nothing.

If anything else happens between the two of you—and I mean anything—we're suspending the both of you. And getting the police involved. This ends now. Hear me?

I nod.

Jamie's been warned. If you even come near him, he's going to turn and walk the other way. And you need to do the same. You got anything to say?

I shake my head.

Good, he says. Get a pass from what's her name and go back to class.

I rise and turn toward the door, but Mr. Kerr says, If you two want to kill each other outside of school, you go right ahead. But not on my watch.

I stop at the door.

For a second, I say, I thought you were doing this because you actually cared.

He opens his mouth but then shuts it. I turn my back on him.

Beth hurries into Algebra class just as the bell is ringing. The teacher gives her a look of annoyance. A seat is open behind me, and Beth walks to it, even though she would be more discreet if she sat near the door. I smile at her, and she smiles at me, and class begins.

About ten minutes into the lecture, as Mrs. Cox is turned to draw equations on the board, I pass Beth a note that says

I won't be in your lunch anymore.
Kerr moved me.

I hear the scribble of Beth's pen behind me, and she passes the note back:

Why?
That asshole.

Mrs. Cox wants us to work on equations, and she wanders the room, checking people's answers. When she is on the other side of the room, helping Billy McMurphy, I say to Beth, He wants to separate me and Jamie.

Beth considers this, and I suspect she thinks this is a good idea but doesn't want to say it aloud.

He said the next time anything happens, he'll suspend both of us.

You believe that? she says.

Yeah.

She corrects herself: I mean, do you believe that Jamie would get suspended too? Or just you?

I don't know.

Beth says, I bet his lawyer daddy would be down here in two seconds, and Jamie wouldn't see one day of suspension.

The lunchroom isn't as full during C period. I used to wish I had C lunch because that's when Craig ate, but now I miss my new friends. I walk toward an empty table, tray in hand. I sit and start to eat, and then I hear a girl's voice yell, Hey, kid. Craig's Brother!

It's Angie, the girl from the river Saturday night. The cheerleader. She's sitting with Danielle, who is wearing the same leather jacket and red boots she wore then.

You want to sit with us? Angie asks.

I rise and pick up my tray.

What are you doing eating in our lunch period? Danielle says.

I tell them that my schedule got changed but don't say why.

What happened to your face? Angie says. Did your brother put a roll of quarters in his hand and hit you too?

I shake my head and say I picked a fight with the doorjamb in my bedroom.

There are three other people at the table, two guys and another girl. I'm not sure of their names and no one introduces me. They all act as if I belong here, even though this isn't the same type of crowd as Luke and Kenny and Dawn and Beth. Their clothes are nicer and the boys' hair is shorter.

Angie asks me where my brother's been.

I don't know where he is.

You mean he just took off?

I nod.

She is very pretty. Black hair pulled back in a ponytail and white teeth that fill her mouth when she smiles. Her skin glows luminescent.

Lunch goes on, and some of the others leave. Angie says she has to stop by the library before class, and the remaining students rise to leave with her.

Well, kid, she says, it was good to see you.

She puts her hand on my shoulder and picks up her tray.

I'm alone.

I have no food left, but I don't rise to leave. I stare at my tray, into the molded plastic squares stained with the slimy leftovers of Jell-O and cream corn and ketchup.

I'm thinking about how things might be okay again. How maybe life can return to some sort of normalcy—not return, because my life was never normal, but change maybe, morph and transform into a somewhat normal life. I've taken the worst Jamie is going to do, and I survived. It was awful—and my body still aches—but I've been through worse. I had told Bell and Kerr that he could never hurt me, and it was true, in a way: there's nothing he could do to me that would be worse than losing my mom. And now maybe he'll leave me alone. I can move on, with Beth and my new friends. And with Craig, if he comes back.

It feels stupid to think I had the gun in my hand this morning, that I thought about bringing it to school.

I just want to put this behind me. I'll convince Craig to put it all behind him too.

With these thoughts, a realization comes over me. If I want to move on, that means I want to live. That means I want things to get better. Despite all that's happened, despite those guys kicking the shit out of me the other day, I can see how good life can be. And just like Mr. James said, I can *try* to make my life better. I have to try.

And I do want to try.

Hey, Danny.

I know who it is before I turn around. It's Gretchen. She sits at the table, with one chair between us.

I feel myself getting tense and I will myself to relax. She isn't worth it.

Hi, Gretchen.

I just wanted to say I'm sorry.

For what?

For what Jamie did. For Craig leaving. For all of it. I'm sorry.

I don't say anything, but she can tell that I'm accepting her apology, although it's not really an apology. Just pity.

The lunchroom is nearly cleared out. The clock shows only a few minutes before the bell rings.

Things have just gotten way out of control, she says. I just don't want anyone else to get hurt.

Neither do I, I say. I grin and add, Well, unless it's Jamie.

She looks at me incredulously then realizes I'm trying to make a joke. She laughs and I laugh with her.

I'm in my last class of the day, sitting in back, looking out the window. The teacher is talking about ancient Greece and the battles between the Athenians and the Spartans.

My mind is an exhausted blank. I'm staring out the window but not paying attention to anything. I'm the gray empty screen of a turned-off television.

There's a relief in this emptiness, a lack of stress. It's Friday; I survived the week. I've lived through all that's happened to me. I've lived through it and I'm going to continue living.

I want to live.

Out the window, the seniors have mostly left. A few lingerers make their way through the parking lot. Jamie's car is gone. So are Dawn's and Doug's. I see the girl Angie and a guy who must be her boyfriend walking from the school. They get into a small white Fiero. He drives. She rides in the passenger seat. I watch, not really paying attention. The car zips out of its space and through the parking lot, quick like an insect. When it gets to the stoplight and stops to wait for green, a Nova pulls into the parking lot.

I sit up, alert.

The Nova starts to make a loop of the parking lot, trolling slowly like some kind of robot on patrol. I can't see the driver. He's just a shape. But the shape looks like Craig. The color of the Nova is right and this car has no dents or stickers that would give it away as a different car. I can't see the license plate, and I don't know Craig's license number anyway. No one else in this school drives a Nova.

The car finishes its loop and then it accelerates, loud enough that I can hear it faintly through the window, and it blows through the yellow light at the entrance to school, the tires chirping audibly as it speeds around the corner and out of sight.

Beth and I are at my locker. The hall is filled with kids, heading toward the bus stop or to the parking lot to wait for their rides. Beth is telling me about something that happened in her art class today, but I'm not listening. I haven't told her yet that I thought I saw Craig's Nova.

Then Dawn is coming down the hall, fast. Her face is red and she is breathing heavy.

Oh, my god, she says. You two have to come with me.

What's going on? Beth says.

Your brother, she says to me, he just beat the shit out of Moose Johnson.

Luke is waiting for us in the car, which is parked by the curb in the loading zone. He gets out and lets me sit in front.

I've never seen anything like that, Dawn says. I'm telling you. He really fucked Moose up.

We're waiting at the light and she thumps her hand against the steering wheel impatiently.

They tell us what happened. They were in Taco Bell, waiting in line. Moose and some other guys—Tracy Goddard and Darren Christensen— were there. I'm not sure who Tracy Goddard is, but I think Darren Christensen must be the kid with the Alabama shirt. Moose and his friends had already been through the line and were sitting and eating. Dawn didn't see Craig pull up. She just saw him coming through the door.

Luke says, I was real excited to see him, so I said hi. He just ignored me and turned in the direction of Moose.

Dawn says Moose looked up and saw Craig. He had a strange look on his face: kind of like he knew Craig was coming for him but he had a real confidence that Craig wouldn't do anything.

He wasn't afraid at all, Luke says.

No, but he should have been, Dawn says. Craig just punched him right in the face. Moose tried to get up, but Craig punched him over and over, and then Moose fell back onto the floor and Craig crouched over him and still kept whaling on him.

He was out cold, Luke says, and Craig was still hitting him.

Dawn and Luke both look unsettled, like they just witnessed a murder.

Tracy Goddard tried to pull Craig off and he shoved him over a table, Dawn says. He literally went clear over the table and fell on the floor on the other side. I thought he was going to break his neck.

And then Craig grabbed Darren Christensen and started yelling at him.

He was holding him like this, Dawn says, gesturing with one hand while keeping the other on the wheel. Yelling at him: *You're lucky I don't do this to you, motherfucker!*

Darren looked like he was about to piss his pants, Luke says.

Then what happened? I say.

He just left, she says. He didn't even look at us when he walked by. Just left. I saw him get into his car and lay rubber getting out of there.

We split, Luke says. The manager was calling the cops. People were freaked the fuck out. I'm telling you: Moose looked like he was dead. There was a puddle of blood. I got a good look. The blood was spreading out in the grooves in the tile.

We've got to find Craig, I say, before he finds Jamie.

Up ahead is Taco Bell. Sheriff's vehicles fill the parking lot. There's an ambulance too.

Dawn drives by slowly. A cruiser has the entrance blocked off, and a uniformed deputy is standing and answering questions of anyone who tries to pull in.

Sergeant Frederickson is talking to an employee—maybe the manager—outside. He looks directly at me, and even though he must be forty or fifty feet away, he makes eye contact.

I turn away and say to Dawn, Keep going.

We drive to my house first. We go inside so Dawn and Luke can call people to see if they've seen him. Beth and I stand in the living room and wait. She is looking around, and I don't want her to see. The beer cans. The ashtray so full that cigarette ash is spilled onto the coffee table like gray gunpowder. The stains on the carpet. The layer of dust on top of the TV and across the gray, mirrored screen.

I tell Beth I'm going to look in Craig's room and see if there is any sign that he came home.

She follows, and we look around. He hasn't been there. I feel like I could sense his presence if he had. The room is just as empty as it's been all week.

I walk back toward the living room, but Beth turns the other way and peeks into my bedroom.

Is this your room? she says.

Yeah.

Down the hall, Dawn is talking to someone, telling the person that if Doug comes home, please tell him that Dawn called.

Beth steps into my room. I stand in the doorway. I hear Dawn punching numbers on the phone. Beth looks at my posters and my cassettes and the bed where I sleep. I don't know what to think of my room. No one has ever bothered to look at it before, and I feel self-conscious of what others might think.

It's nice, she says.

I wish I were showing it to her under other circumstances. I wish it was just the two of us—and we weren't searching for Craig—and Beth and I could hang out like we did the first time I visited her house. Just hang out and talk and play music.

Hey, Dawn shouts from down the hall.

Beth and I walk back, and Dawn says they couldn't reach anyone.

We drive back through town, looking in the parking lots of the IGA and the gas stations. The ambulance is gone from Taco Bell, but two police cars are still there. We drive by Gretchen's apartment, just in case. Then we drive down to the river where the fire was the other night and Craig pointed the gun at Gretchen.

We get out of the car, but there's no use. No one is here. The place looks different during the day. The light has done something to change it, and it lacks the mystery and the allure from Saturday night. The fire barrel sits without a fire, rusted a dark burnt-red. The water of the river is murky brown. The trees are naked and the ground is layered with wet, hard-packed leaves. I don't see any animals, not even a bird. The sunlight is harsh.

I look to where I think the cars were, to where the fight happened, and try to find where I was standing and where Craig was. I look at the ground, like a forensics investigator looking for tracks. But there's no evidence of what happened. None that I can find.

There's one of those goddamn quarters, Dawn says, leaning down.

She's a good ten feet away. I'm not even looking in the right spot.

I stare where she is, and now I think I can see it. The place where Jamie's Camaro was parked. The place where Craig and Gretchen were screaming. The place where Jamie was lying on the ground.

Shit, I say.

I look up at Dawn and Luke and Beth.

What? Beth says.

We should go by Jamie's house.

Dawn turns onto Mabry Street, and immediately we hear sirens behind us. A police car is there, as if out of nowhere, and Dawn signals and begins to pull over, but the car doesn't wait. It's out and around us and speeding away as if we are standing still.

We approach the houses around Monroe Village subdivision, and Beth asks which house is Jamie's.

I think it's that one, Dawn says, slowing the car.

I tell her she's right.

The house sits there as it did before, rich and opulent. No sign of Jamie's Camaro. No sign of Craig's Nova.

Another siren behind us. Dawn pulls over onto a side street, and the police car flies past, lights flashing.

Something's going on up there, Dawn says matter-of-factly.

Let's go look, I say.

Beth says, You don't think...?

I don't know, I say.

But I do know what I'm thinking and it's the same thing Beth is thinking. Dawn pulls out without protest because now we're all thinking it.

We're silent, the four of us, but a tension is in the air of the car, like some kind of invisible feeling is rising from all of us, like steam in cold air. Now the car is full of it, this dreadful unnamed feeling.

Up ahead we see a cluster of flashing lights. A trail of cars is backed up, keeping us from getting close.

Flares light the road, closing our lane, with a couple of uniformed deputies in the road, waving the other lane through and holding our lane. I can't count how many police cars there are. There is a fire truck and an ambulance.

Pull over, I say.

I open the door as the car rolls to a stop. The air has a toxic burnt-rubber smell. I walk fast down the shoulder. Beth is behind me, and farther back still are Dawn and Luke.

I crest the small hill at the top of Dead Man's Curve and look down into the field on the other side. I take in what I see in a blur of confusion. Cops. Paramedics. A helicopter parked in the field like it belongs there. And a car, crumpled like a soda can, upside down at least a hundred feet from the road. The car is smoking, blackened, wet as if just extinguished.

Giant gouges of fresh soil torn up from the frozen ground lie in its path. The car must have rolled ten times.

Jamie is talking to a police officer on the side of the road. His Camaro is parked farther down on the shoulder. I see a person on a stretcher, and paramedics carrying it to the helicopter. Hurrying. Focused. Smoke rises from the body.

Oh, my god, Danny, Beth says.

She is next to me, crying.

What? I say.

So much is happening. Time has slowed down and sped up all at once. Realization comes to me in stages.

The car. Even smoking and smashed, I recognize it.

The person on the stretcher, being lifted into the helicopter. Black-burnt clothes. Tendrils of smoke still rising in the cold. Face covered in an oxygen mask. Still I can tell. Just from the shape.

Craig.

I'm running toward the paramedics. I hear someone screaming and know it's me, but I don't feel myself doing it and can't stop myself.

Beth yells my name.

The cops see me now, and one runs in to stop me. He grabs me, and I push him, and he falls and rolls down the hill, backwards-somersaulting. And then another cop is in front of me, and I raise my fist, but he's saying my name, over and over. His face takes shape out of a blur. It's Frederickson.

He wraps his arms around me, and all my strength is gone. I push against him, but I am weak, and then I let him hold me. Over his shoulder, a paramedic swings the helicopter door shut.

I hear the screaming—my screaming—die in my throat.

We're standing—Beth, Dawn, Luke, and me—at the edge of the road. Sergeant Frederickson is there. My hands are trembling, my legs shaking.

The helicopter is not moving, and I don't know why. They're in there. Craig. The paramedics.

Why aren't they leaving? Dawn says. Jesus Christ.

The blades start to move, slowly at first, gaining speed. Cold air pushes against us, and debris—dust and blades of dead grass.

Here, Frederickson says, you kids get behind this car.

He gestures to a police cruiser.

It's about to get real windy, he says.

The others walk around the car, and I do too, but it's because my legs seem to move on their own. I'm not controlling them.

The wind blows faster and colder, and all the people around are ducking behind cars. Dirt and sticks pelt the car. My eyes water as I stare over the hood. The blades whirl faster and faster, and I think they must be going fast enough, but the speed increases more and more, and the wind against my face is a steady gush of cold air.

And then the helicopter is off the ground, just floating there like magic because now that it's up it seems no matter how fast the blades are spinning this shouldn't be possible.

It lifts higher and higher, the truth of its wind blowing against me. And then it's up past the trees and flying away.

I don't know how I know, but I do. Craig is dead.

Is your dad at work? Frederickson says.

I'm looking away. Jamie is sitting in a police cruiser down the road with another cop.

Why don't you come with me and we'll tell him what happened?

I can't believe that life goes on. That there are things I'm supposed to do.

Come on, Danny, he says, placing a hand on my shoulder.

Okay.

Beth hugs me. She and Dawn and Luke are all crying. Dawn says something, but I don't hear it.

Call me, Beth says. When you know something. It doesn't matter how late.

I feel myself nodding, and I don't know who is controlling me because my brain seems to have been turned off. I'm not thinking. I'm just blank. Beth hugs me again, and I hold her with limp, numb arms.

Frederickson is talking to another officer, telling him what he's going to do.

It's too much for one family, I hear him say. God ought to be ashamed.

He comes over and opens the car door for me, and I slide in and sit on the leather seat. I look at Beth through the glass and think about how I'm sitting in a car and how the metal and glass around me can be smashed like a can in a fist. I imagine what it was like for Craig as the car was rolling, caving in around him, trapping him inside as it began to burn.

Beth holds her hand to the window, her face contorted from crying, and I reach up, but Frederickson pulls away. And she's behind us and gone.

We pull past the car Jamie is in. Now he is alone.

He looks up at me. I stare at him. I don't try to tell him anything with my look. My mind is too blank for that right now. His face looks shell-shocked, like he doesn't even know who he's looking at.

Chatter comes from the cruiser's CB, and Frederickson turns the volume down so it's a low background static.

He tells me that Jamie said Craig was chasing him. That Craig had pulled up next to him while he was driving and started waving a gun at him. Jamie took off and Craig chased him. Craig rear-ended him a couple times, jolting him hard enough to break a rear light and loosen the bumper, and Jamie accelerated and accelerated, trying to get away. They raced through the streets, and Jamie said he took Dead Man's Curve as fast as he could. Frederickson doesn't call it that—he doesn't use the word dead—but that's what he's referring to as he tells the story. When Craig hit the curve, trying to stick with Jamie, he lost control.

His tires slid out from under him, Frederickson says. When I got there....

He stops and doesn't finish what he was going to say.

He doesn't bother to tell me about Moose Johnson and all that happened at Taco Bell. And he doesn't ask me if I know what all of this was about. I expect him to, but he doesn't.

Frederickson pulls into the parking lot at Dad's work, a gravel runway linking manufacturing plants and warehouses. Time seems like it has a mind of its own because it can't be more than four o'clock and yet dusk seems to be settling over us. The air is darkening. Frederickson's lights are on, the beams cutting through the gray in front of us.

I keep remembering what I saw. Like the spasms of pain I've felt since Jamie and his friends beat me up. Only the spasms are in my brain.

Is it this one? Frederickson asks.

Yes.

I hear myself say it, but the voice doesn't sound like me, and I don't remember moving my lips.

I've been through this before, with Mom, and I remember how it was at first and how it was later. I wish I could skip the now and get to the later. But I feel guilty for wanting to skip the mourning. Or skip the worst of it. I couldn't skip it all.

We walk to the entrance to the building. Inside, the shop seems cavernous, the muted colors of concrete and steel inside the gloom. The walls are lined with pipe, ten and twenty feet long. Some dark and brown, like the earth. Some silver, like Dad's gun. A forklift moves in the distance. The flashpoint of an arc welder at the back of the shop. A few guys stand near a pallet of scrap, talking and smoking, their hands black with soot, just like Dad's are when he comes home.

They look at us with skepticism—a kid and a cop—and then one of them recognizes me.

Hey, he says, which one are you? Craig or Danny?

I can't speak.

You looking for your dad?

He points toward the flash of welding light.

We start that way. Light bulbs in the ceiling pool light at the floor, like steps on a path. Up ahead, the fire from the welder gets brighter, showering sparks.

Don't look directly at the light, I say.

We're ten feet away, but Dad hasn't seen us. He's concentrating on the weld he's making. The helmet covers his face. Thick gloves over his hands. But I can tell it's him.

Dad! I yell.

He looks up, and I wonder what he can see through the black lens. Just blurry dark images. Like what I was seeing outside—dusk before dusk.

A four-inch flame shoots from the welder, and then he turns it off. The fire extinguishes with a pop. He flips the front of his mask up and looks at us with what seems like a sense of resignation. He sets the welder down on the machine it's connected to with wires. He moves with slow, methodical patience. He lifts the mask off and holds it in his arms like a football helmet while Frederickson and I step forward. He doesn't say anything. He just waits for it.

When Frederickson tells him that Craig's been in a car accident and taken by Care Flight to the hospital, he takes the news with seeming indifference. It's as if he expected this conversation, expected it for years and it's long overdue. Frederickson says that the helicopter was taking him to Grand Valley hospital and he would be happy to drive us there.

I'll drive us, Dad says.

I'll be honest, Frederickson says, it doesn't look good.

Dad sets the helmet on the machine. He takes off the thick welding gloves—blackened with grime—and sets them beside the helmet. His eyes focus on the weld he was making, a gray-butter seam between two pipes. The weld is unfinished. His eyes are looking at it but his brain is not.

He looks up at Frederickson.

Did you see him? Dad asks Frederickson.

Yes.

Did you? he says to me.

I hear my mouth saying, It was hard to recognize him.

Now Dad's expression changes. The blood drains out of his face, and his skin goes pale. He fumbles for his pack of cigarettes in his breast pocket, and his hands tremble.

You sure you don't want me to take you? Frederickson asks.

Dad waits until he's lit his cigarette, taken a long drag, and exhaled before he speaks.

No, go on. You've done enough.

Frederickson opens his mouth to speak.

Go on! Dad barks. Get out of here.

He gestures with his arm in a flinging, shooing motion.

Danny, you stay with me, Dad says.

Frederickson tells us both that if we need anything to call him. He starts in a turning motion, and it feels like something more should be said but I don't know what it is. Frederickson's back is to me and he's walking toward the door.

Come on, Dad says.

I follow him to the locker room. I sit on the bench and wait, wrapped in the green coat. He washes his hands, using the half-circle sink I always thought was neat when I was a kid. You step on the metal pipe on the floor and the water comes out like a fountain. That's what I called it when I was a kid: a fountain. I remember Craig and me taking turns stepping on the trigger and letting the water spray out. I haven't thought of that in years, but here it is, a memory of Craig: just a boy, smiling, happy.

In the truck, Dad lights a cigarette and fills the cab with its smoke. When he smokes it to the filter, he stubs it out in the overflowing ashtray. He waits only a few seconds and lights another.

It's dark now, and the highway is crowded with rush-hour traffic. I look out the window, watching the cars we pass and the ones that pass us. I look at the people inside. None of them have any idea what happened. I try to understand how such a world-ending event can occur and no one even notices.

Dad and I don't speak a word on the drive to the hospital.

He circles the building, looking for the ER. When he finds it, he parks. He does all this with no sense of urgency. As if he is calm or numb. I feel it too, as we walk through the lot toward the lit-up glass doors. My steps are robotic. An autopilot has taken over.

Inside, a man and woman sit with a small boy, who is laboring to breathe. Another teen sits with his mom, cradling a swollen arm. An old man with an oxygen tank sits alone. A man the size of Moose Johnson sits with a woman, looking worried. The man looks like an older version of Moose, and it takes me a few moments to understand why Moose Johnson's father would be here.

Dad approaches the counter and tells a nurse with acne on her face who he is and who we're here to see. She tells him to wait a moment. We stand and wait, and she says, You can sit over there, sir.

I'll wait here, Dad says.

We stand. Statues. We make the woman uncomfortable, and she calls three times asking for someone to come talk to us.

Finally, a doctor comes. He is younger than Dad with short-cropped black hair and glasses and a white coat. He asks if Dad will come with him. Dad tells me to wait, but I follow them anyway. We don't go far. As soon as we're through the double-doors and into a hall away from the waiting room, the doctor turns and talks.

He says, I'm sorry, but your son has passed.

Dad starts to breathe fast, the air wheezing in and out. He's trying to control himself but he can't control his breathing.

Unfortunately, the doctor says, he never made it to the hospital. He died in the helicopter on the way here. There was nothing that could be done. He was too damaged from the crash.

Damaged? Dad says.

The doctor swallows and says, The injuries were too severe.

Dad forcibly slows his breathing. He looks down, collecting himself. He looks back at the doctor.

I want to see him.

Sir, that's not possible right now. Later, the police might want to....

Dad waits for him to finish his sentence, but he doesn't. He probably has to tell people this kind of news all the time, but not people like my dad.

I will see him, Dad says. Now.

The doctor says he'll see what he can arrange. He asks us to stay in the waiting room, and Dad moves in that direction reluctantly. The nurse at the station looks at us, and Dad glares at her as if this is all her fault. She turns away.

We sit, and a few minutes later the man who is the size of Moose Johnson rises out of his seat and approaches us. He asks if Dad is Craig's father. Dad says yes, and then the man takes a deep breath and says, My boy's in surgery right now because of your son.

Dad doesn't flinch or acknowledge the comment in any way.

Before your son went after Jamie, he says, he attacked my boy. For no reason. Just attacked him.

I stand up. I lift up my coat and my shirt and I say, See this?

He looks down at the bruises and welts on my ribs and chest. I drop my shirt and point to my face.

Your son did this. Him and Jamie, I say, and I don't want my voice to keep rising, but it does.

Dad stands and puts a hand on my chest because I'm moving forward even though I don't mean to.

My brother is dead because of your son, I say. Your son is a fucking murderer!

Now Dad pulls me away, and I let him.

The woman at the front desk is on the telephone, looking nervously at us. Every face in the waiting room is turned toward us.

Stay right here, Dad says.

He speaks calmly.

Stay, he says again.

He turns and walks back to Moose Johnson's father.

When I was younger, my father was a tower, strong and wiry. He is smaller now, dwarfed by the thickness of Moose Johnson's father. But Mr. Johnson looks scared and Dad does not.

Dad looks him in the eyes and says, Stay away from my son. Stay away from me. This is your only warning.

They lock eyes for a moment, and then Dad walks back toward me. Mr. Johnson watches him and turns back to his wife, who stands in the background with her hands clutched to her chest.

Fucking white trash, Mr. Johnson says over his shoulder.

Dad ignores him.

A security guard comes through the double doors. The woman at the desk points and the guard comes up to us. He isn't much older than Craig and probably not any taller than I was in sixth grade.

Is there a problem here? he says.

Dad looks at him, and I can see his patience is all used up.

Yes there is, Dad says.

Well, what is it?

My son's dead, Dad says loudly so everyone around can hear. I'm waiting to go see his body. That's a problem for me, but that ain't got a fucking thing to do with you.

The guard recoils. He backs away and raises his arms in surrender.

I'm sorry, sir.

He walks over to the counter and begins talking to the woman there in a hushed voice. They glance at us and talk, and then the guard stands nearby, saying nothing and trying not to look scared.

Let's go wait outside, Dad says.

He lights a cigarette, and we stand in the cold. The night feels as black as can be. The streetlamps and the car headlights can't illuminate it. I close my eyes and lean against a pillar and smell Dad's smoke and I take stock of all that's happened and I can't believe it. I just can't believe it. Like Frederickson said: it's too much for one family. If you could even call what's left a family.

Small flakes of snow drift in the air.

Someone in a lab coat, someone new, comes outside and tells Dad that he can show him Craig.

Dad drops the cigarette on the pavement and steps on it.

The man, a chubby man with round cheeks that are speckled with red because of the cold, looks back and forth between Dad and me and says, This is nothing for a boy to see.

Dad looks at me, looks back at the man.

He's seen it before, Dad says. He can come if he wants.

Craig is under a white sheet, which looks yellowish in the fluorescent light. All the color in the room looks off. Dad's face, which looked calm earlier, just looks haggard now. The light changes his face somehow, lifts its camouflage.

The air smells of smoke and a new acrid odor I've never smelled before. Burnt hair and burnt flesh.

The man reaches delicately over the sheet, taking it in two hands, lifting and pulling it back, and laying it across Craig's chest in a perfect fold.

Dad gasps and I reel on my feet, every part of the world spinning except Craig.

He's recognizable but only barely. Most of his hair is gone, and what's left looks like tufts of black feathers poking out from the blistered dome of his skull. His skin is red and black and bubbled up in a hard crust. One side of his face is burnt worse than the other, like his skin there was made of candle wax that began to melt away before hardening again. His eye socket seems to have shifted places, sliding sideways and toward his brow, with a hint of the eye visible, gray like a smoked windowpane. The other eye is closed. His eyebrows are gone, and eyelashes. His mouth is pulled open in a sneer showing his teeth, the white standing out against the rest of the colors. The tip of a pink tongue sticks out between his bite, dried and swollen but not burned.

Dad turns away, and when I don't, Dad tells the hospital employee to cover Craig back up.

That's enough, Dad says.

And then Craig is hidden behind the white sheet again, but I will see him for the rest of my life. How he was at the end. Just as I see Mom.

Driving home, we pass a bank with the time lit up in red digits. It says it's 8:45. I stare at the numbers because it feels like midnight, like 1:30 in the morning, like some point in the middle of the night when time slows and it seems like the day will never come. The streets are almost empty.

Snow is coming down. Enough that Dad flips the windshield wipers, just one screeching skate across the glass and then he turns them off. He does it again in another twenty or thirty seconds.

The snow falls faster. Its flakes light up in the headlights of the truck. Each one could be a star or a planet, some object in the sky. Comets sailing through space. And our planet could be a sun in their solar systems. If it's true that some suns are big enough that our planet is only the size of a snowflake comparatively, then maybe earth is in the icy dust around one of those snowflakes.

Or maybe each flake is a person. Or every star is a person. A soul in the universe. Or maybe nothing means anything. Maybe we aren't really here at all. We're figments of the imagination of something somewhere. Just thoughts. Not even real.

Goddamn him, Dad says.

It's a mutter at first then he growls it, teeth clenched. Goddamn him!

He stops at the drive-through and buys a case of beer and a bottle of George Dickel. The alcohol sits on the seat between us.

Get me a beer, would you? he says.

I pull open the side of the box and hand him a can. He cracks its seal and takes a long drink, keeping his eyes on the road.

Dad speaks again, but this time he's not angry.

Do you remember when you were a kid, he says, and the four of us would pile into this truck when we had to go somewhere?

I don't answer because it's not really a question. I remember of course: the four of us on the bench seat of the truck.

Your mom would sit over by the door, he says, and you'd be next to her. When you were a baby, she'd carry you, but later, you'd sit next to her. Craig would be over here by me. Sometimes he'd lean into me, like I was reading him a story, and I'd put my arm around him.

He's quiet for a few seconds as the wipers screech against the windshield.

I remember we went to a picnic once down by the levy, he says. He laughs, just a little, and adds, You were crying, and your brother went chasing after a bee and got himself stung, and your mom and I ended up getting into a big fight. But on the drive there, in the truck, we were all happy.

If there's a heaven, he says, I want to go back to that moment. Us in the truck. Driving. Beautiful summer day. You boys sitting between us. Everyone happy.

He finishes his beer and asks for another one. After he takes a drink, he says, Of course, if that moment in the truck is my heaven, I guess this one's my hell.

Dad finishes three beers before we get home. He goes to the kitchen and pours the Dickel into a glass.

The answering machine light is flashing, red like the hazards on a car.

I press the button.

The first message is Frederickson, telling us that he'll come by on Saturday to talk about a few things and saying that if we need anything in the meantime we should call.

The second is Mr. James from school, saying he heard the news and he was sorry and he wanted to know if there was anything he could do.

The third call is Beth.

I'm so sorry, she says. *Please call if you want to talk. It doesn't matter how late.*

She pauses as if she wants to say more but can't think what to say, and so she hangs up.

I stare at the phone. Dad sits down in his chair and takes a long swig of the whiskey. He chases it with a gulp of beer. He turns on the TV and stares at the screen, but I can tell he doesn't even know what he's watching.

I walk back to Craig's room. I turn on the light. I sit on the edge of the bed. I look around. I curl up in a ball and lay my head on his pillow. I smell him. The last time I saw him, in the car before school, he told me he loved me and I didn't say it back. Now the blankness inside of me cracks and breaks open, and I can feel myself starting to cry. And once it comes, it comes in a flood. I bury my face in his pillow, and I cry and I sob. When I'm finally finished, the pillow is so wet with tears and snot and saliva that I have to flip it over. I lay my head down, and the pillow is cool on my cheek.

I sleep hard for a few hours, but I wake up in panic. I'm fully clothed, still in Craig's bed. It feels wrong, like I'm in his grave.

I walk down the hall. Dad's passed out on the couch. The room is dark except for the blue-white light of the TV. Cans stand on the coffee table like tombstones. The bottle of Dickel is half empty.

I turn off the TV and go to my room, leaving Dad where he is. The sheets are cold, and I shiver until I warm up, but even then I can't feel comfortable. I turn over and turn back. I go in and out of sleep. I wake thinking it's a nightmare only to remember it's not. Memories and dreams intertwine and mix, like paint drops in water, spreading and fading and diluting until it's impossible to tell one from the other.

When the room starts to lighten from the soft glow, I sit up and have to think what day it is. Saturday. I can sleep in. I wonder—only for an instant—if Craig has to work this morning and whether I will hear him getting ready to leave. Then I remember all that's happened.

And I see Craig's face, burned like someone held a welding torch to it.

Dad is asleep on the couch in the same position. The house is cold, but he doesn't seem to notice. His chest barely rises. His hair is greasy and disheveled. His cheeks peppered with stubble. Yellowing skin. Hands rough and calloused. Dead skin on chapped lips. Wrinkles around his eyes, crow's feet so deep it's as if they were carved with a knife. And dark circles a sick grayish-purple—a lifetime of exhaustion.

I walk to the front and look out the window and see the empty space where the Nova is usually parked. I think of the car, smashed and crumpled like a wadded piece of paper. I think of Craig. I can't stop thinking of Craig. I wish I could think of anything else but Craig.

I pull the phone down the hall to Craig's room. I sit on the floor and lean against his bed and look at his posters and wait for Beth to answer.

Danny? she says.

Yeah, I say. It's me.

Oh, my god. I'm so sorry.

Thank you, I say.

I feel inside that I'm thawing and splitting and breaking, like tectonic plates are grinding up against one another. I don't want to cry.

How did you hear? I say.

It was on the news. They didn't release the name but.... She pauses then says, Obviously I already knew who it was.

I say nothing.

Are you okay? she says. I mean, I'm sorry. I know you're not okay.

You're right, I say, feeling relieved that I can say this. I feel like I'll never be okay again.

I cry into the phone, unable to stop my heaving breaths, my loud sobs.

She talks about how life has to go on for me and how I'm going to be okay. It takes time to heal. She tells me that she's here for me.

But there are things I can't tell her. I can't tell her that she's not enough. I can't tell her that I don't want to live anymore. That it was too hard before and now it's going to be worse. Much worse.

Beth offers to come over, but I say that's not a good idea. She asks if I want to come over to her house.

My mom won't care, she says. She knows what happened.

Maybe later, I say.

What are you going to do? she asks.

Dad will take care of everything, I say. When he wakes up, he'll call the funeral home. He's good about that stuff, doing what has to be done. He's always been like that. He gets drunk every night, but he never misses a day of work.

I don't say that after Mom's death, he went through the paperwork and police reports and talked with the insurance company about why they wouldn't pay. He was like a robot, doing all the tangible things that had to be taken care of but hardly talking at all to Craig and me.

I don't know how we'll afford all this, I say. There won't be any insurance money. The Nova only had liability, I say. And they'd fight it even if—

Beth breaks in. No, Danny. I mean, what are *you* going to do?

I don't know.

I go to the bathroom and strip down and look at my bruises and welts in the mirror. They're starting to fade. It still hurts to breathe. My muscles still feel like weights. But all of that pain has somehow been numbed. My head aches, as if grief has manifested into physical pain.

I stare at myself. I hate myself. I wish it had been me.

I make the water as hot as I can take, and I stand under the spray, leaning against the porcelain until the water begins to cool.

In my bedroom—my body warm against the chill of the room—I pull on jeans and stand shirtless in front of my closet. Finally, I go through my dirty clothes and pull out the Judas Priest shirt Craig gave me, which still smells faintly of campfire.

I put on Dad's green coat, and I pull the Magnum out from under the mattress. I slide it in the inside pocket, and it fits. The coat pulls on that side, but it's impossible to tell what the object is. When I put my hands in the outside pockets, you can't tell there's anything at all in there.

I stop in the living room on my way out. Dad is sleeping in the same position. I stare at him for a long time. Then I walk over to him and kiss him on the forehead.

Good-bye, Dad.

When I step outside, a car is sitting in the parking space where Craig's Nova used to sit. I don't recognize it at first and then I do. A beat-up Toyota Cressida, it's Gretchen's car. She's sitting in the front seat.

I walk into the yard and she gets out and asks if she can talk to me. The crisp morning air is sharp like a knife. I walk over leaves matted and layered across the brown grass. The snow from last night barely stuck, but the ground is wet and the trees gleam with sheens of ice.

I was going to knock, she says, but it's so early I didn't want to wake you.

I say nothing.

I'm so sorry, Danny.

She starts to cry, as if she's been holding it back. Loud gasps of breath smoke into the cold air.

Can we sit in the car? she squeaks.

She opens her door, and I walk around. It's almost warm inside. She turns the ignition and let's warm air pump into the compartment.

She says, I don't know how all this happened, Danny.

Now she is crying again, her hands at her face.

I feel like this is all my fault, she says.

He needed new tires, I say.

It's my fault he was chasing after Jamie, she says.

It's Jamie's fault he was chasing after Jamie, I say.

I almost say that it's not her fault but my fault, but I stop myself. She would tell me not to blame myself. But I know. I could have stopped it from happening. If I hadn't told him about being beaten up, he would be alive. That's the simple truth.

I stare out the window. The sun is still low, still beginning its rise, and the world has a crisp but not fully lit look to it. It's as if the sun is shining through a special filter today that softens it, that mutes it. Like adjusting the tint on a television set.

Gretchen says, Jamie's really sorry, Danny. About everything.

The weight of the Magnum rests against my stomach.

Have you talked to him? I ask.

Last night, she says. On the phone. I couldn't see him.

What do you mean you couldn't see him?

I just couldn't, she says. I couldn't bring myself to see his face. It was like...I don't know.

I wait.

When I broke up with your brother, being with Jamie, it didn't feel like I was doing anything wrong. But last night, when he wanted to see me, it felt like cheating.

Craig's dead, I say.

I know, she says. But I kept feeling like I wanted to see Craig, not Jamie. That's why I drove over here. It was like I thought I could go back to him. When I saw his car was gone, it really sunk in.

She smiles at me with an embarrassed, self-aware smile.

Gretchen, I say, what do you want from me?

She swallows.

Do you want me to feel sorry for you? I say.

No, I...

She fumbles for her words.

I just wanted, I don't know, to be around someone who loved your brother as much as I did.

I glare at her and clench my jaw.

As much as you did? I say.

I didn't mean it like that, she says.

I should have let Craig kill you, you fucking bitch.

Danny, I didn't mean...

I don't know what he ever saw in you, I say. The world would be a better place if you had died instead of him.

Her face is cracking, and more tears are coming.

Go ahead and cry, I say. That bullshit might have worked with him or with Jamie, but *I* don't feel sorry for you. The world was better with Craig in it. Is it better with you in it?

Is it better with you in it? she shrieks.

I'm breathing heavy. I look down.

No, I say. It's not.

I open the door and step out into the cold. I slam the door so hard behind me that it rocks the Cressida. She sobs as I walk away.

I walk down the street for a hundred yards or so, and when I hear the whine of Gretchen's car backing out of the driveway, I cut into someone's yard and head to the field behind the houses. When she passes behind me I don't look back. The dirt is glazed with ice, and each step crunches. My shoes are wet, and my toes go from cold to on fire.

The sky is gray from one horizon to the other, like a dull iron lid has been placed over the world.

It takes a long time, but I walk to Mabry Street. I walk on the roadway for a while and then climb up into the trees and walk parallel to it. When I get close to Jamie's house, I go deeper. I stop and watch the house, hidden in the woods. The Camaro sits out front. The breeze sings through the trees in a haunting song. I shiver but I make myself wait.

I imagine walking to the door and ringing the bell. I see Jamie answering. I see the look on his face. Surprise. Shame. I'd pull out the gun. I imagine what comes next in every possible way. Jamie opens his mouth to say something and I shoot him, one bullet after another. Or Jamie tries to slam the door shut and I shoot through it. I kick it open and see that my bullets found their way. He is slumped against the foyer wall, blood leaking from his wounds, gurgling from his mouth. Or I would have to pursue him through the house, shooting him in the back and knocking him forward onto the kitchen floor.

But I also see the door opening and someone else coming to answer, Jamie's dad maybe, or his mom. I would push my way in and pull out the gun and hold it to the person's head and say, Where is Jamie?

I wait and wait, and still there's no movement from the house. No cars coming or going. No flash of light from behind a window. I think more and more about what would happen if someone else answered the door and how I don't really want to kill Jamie's parents.

I'm shivering badly, and I need to move to warm up, so I turn away from Jamie's house and walk through the woods toward town. I leave the trees and walk along the property line between two houses and get to a residential road. The gun's steel is cold inside my coat.

Hours go by, and I walk with no direction. My body shivers at first, but the shivering ceases. The burning in my toes turns to numbness. My hands are claws. My hair becomes crispy, frozen by the cold. My ribs and leg and face—all the places bruised by Jamie's assault—respond differently to the cold, like the meat is rotting there.

I step into stores and restaurants to get out of the cold, and everywhere I go the places seem empty. Like a deep grieving has fallen over the whole community, but I know that's not true. No one cared about Craig. It's just the cold on a Saturday morning that is keeping people in.

I walk into Taco Bell to eat and look around for evidence of what Craig did, but there's no sign that anything happened. I order food, but when the red ground beef peers out of from the shell of the burrito, my stomach clenches and I can't take a bite. I sit for a long time, the food untouched, my feet changing temperature as they thaw. I pull the rest of the money Craig gave me out of my pocket and lay the stack of bills on the table. A little less than a hundred dollars. I won't need it anymore.

When a carload of students from school pulls up and faces I recognize walk into the restaurant, I rise to leave. They look at me and whisper. As I walk by, Stephanie from the principal's office looks at me and says, Danny, I just wanted to say—

I walk out the door without stopping.

I stare out over the field at Dead Man's Curve. The ground is torn up with deep gouges from where the Nova rolled, and there are truck tracks from whatever they used to haul it out. I walk down and look through the black burn scar. I think I'll find a cassette or a can of Kodiak or maybe the cursive metal letters—Nova—that were attached to the fender. Maybe some burnt money. Or Dad's .38. But there's nothing like that—just broken glass and little pieces of metal.

The ground is scorched black like someone built a bonfire here and it burned so hot that there aren't any coals or ashes left. Over time, all evidence of what happened will be erased. It seems like there should be some artifact that should tell the story. But Craig is dead so the memory of what happened—the memory of the person it happened to—doesn't even exist. It only exists in the minds of the rest of us, but we live in different worlds altogether from Craig. His story is over and can never be read.

A police cruiser pulls onto the shoulder at Dead Man's Curve.

Sergeant Frederickson gets out of the car and shouts down to me, I thought I might find you here. Why don't you get in for a minute?

I pause and think and then I do as he asks.

Inside, the car is warm, but my body is still cold, like it's frozen and would take a long time to thaw.

I stopped by your house, he says. Your dad was worried about you.

I say nothing.

Danny, he says, I'm sorry about Craig.

He says it with earnestness, and that's what hurts the most. It makes me think that maybe I can't go through with what I want to do. Because people out there care about me, how can I do what I'm planning to do?

What was my dad doing? I say.

The window is fogging from the warmth.

Making arrangements, Frederickson says. I'm not sure it's fully hit him yet. Like the arrangements can keep him focused. Your dad has a real no-nonsense way about him. He does what has to be done.

I say nothing.

What about you, Danny? he says. What have you been doing? You been here all day?

Not all day.

What have you been doing?

Just wandering around, I say. I don't know what else to do.

I keep waiting for him to mention that he knows I took Dad's gun, but he doesn't.

Your dad was worried about you.

You said that already.

Your guidance counselor from school stopped by too.

I wish everyone would just leave me alone.

I don't look at him. I wipe the fogging window and stare down at the black spot where the Nova burned.

Frederickson says, We all just want to help, Danny, we're—

Can I go now? I say.

He leans back and thinks hard and says, I don't want you to be alone right now, Danny.

I stare at him and I want my eyes to hurt him. His emotions squirm under his skin, but he doesn't back down.

Then will you take me somewhere? I say. I don't want to go home.

Where?

A friend's house, I say. Where you took me before.

Okay, he says, but you have to call your dad and tell him where you are.

He turns toward the windshield and adjusts the heater so it will defrost. A small hole of vision appears at the bottom of the glass and slowly grows, eating the fog.

He puts the car in drive and says, Put on your seatbelt.

Outside of Beth's house, he parks the car on the street and says, Wait a second.

He's working the words around in his head, trying to think of how to say what he wants to say.

I don't want you doing anything stupid, he says. Not today. Not tomorrow. Not next week.

Like what? I say.

But I know what he means, and he gives me a look that says the same thing.

Don't do anything to those you might blame for this, he says. And don't do anything to yourself.

Tears pool against my eyes, but not from sadness. From anger.

You're going to get through this, Danny. I know it doesn't seem like you will, but you will. Don't do anything that's going to...

He shakes his head.

I don't have the words, he says. I just don't want to see you end up on a path like your mom or your brother.

Craig didn't kill himself, I say.

He stares at me and says softly, Your brother was self-destructive. He didn't kill himself, but he is to blame—not someone else—for what happened to him. I'm sorry but that's—

Can I go now? I snap. Or am I under arrest?

Danny, I'm your friend.

My heart is pounding and I can't help but raise my voice. I say to him, almost in a shout, The next time you want to talk to me, *friend*, you're going to have to fucking arrest me. I'm through with your bullshit!

Danny, he says.

But I'm out the door and I slam it behind me and stomp up the walkway to Beth's house. I wish I could compose myself somehow before I knock on the door, but I know Frederickson is watching and he won't leave until I'm inside.

Beth's mom answers the door, and she has a look of sympathy. I put on a friendly face. Beth walks into the foyer and sees me, and I break down. I start crying, and she hugs me. Her mom leaves us alone. I lean into her and she holds me. I hate myself and I hate the world, and Beth is the only good thing left in it.

But I make sure not to lean into her too much. I don't want her to feel the gun.

Beth tells me that I'm freezing and offers to make me some tea. I've never had tea before, but I say yes. I'm alone in her bedroom, so I take off the coat. I fold it up, wrapping the bulky fabric around the gun, and set it on the floor. I change my mind and slide it under the bed because I don't want her picking it up and moving it. I don't want her to see it.

She has a box of tissues on her vanity, and I take one and blow my nose.

I sit on the edge of the bed and stare at the floor. I feel like I'm underwater, like the world around me has changed and all my senses are different now, muffled by the thick air.

My toes burn as blood runs back into them. I take off my shoes. My socks are wet from the tip to halfway up my foot. I take them off too. I wiggle my red toes.

Beth comes in with the tea and says, My god, how long were you out there? It's freezing.

She hands me the tea, and I wrap my hands around it and feel the warmth and sit there and hold it for a long time, watching the ghost tendrils of steam rise, like souls rising and dissipating before finding any sort of heaven.

We say very little. We sit upright on the bed, leaning against pillows, our feet under the blanket. Beth puts in an AC/DC cassette and turns it low to muffle the sound of the TV from the living room. It always seemed like AC/DC needed to be loud, but the music has a grungy, bluesy quality I never noticed before, and when the volume is down low, the fist-pumping rock anthems sound somehow mournful, like sad blues ballads.

Eventually we slide down and pull the covers up, and Beth puts her arms around me, and I feel safe. And I feel like maybe I could be all right. The rage in me seems to have been pulled out, like Beth's presence is enough to withdraw an invisible poison out of my blood through my skin.

I watch as the glimpse of sunlight out the window turns from yellow to orange to red and finally disappears. The sky is black outside. Somehow I've survived one day without my brother.

Beth's mom makes dinner, and Beth brings two plates into her bedroom for us. I eat a little. Corn and mashed potatoes and about half of the broiled chicken breast on my plate. I think briefly of Craig's face when the guy pulled the sheet back, and I have to stop eating. I look at Beth and I push my mind away from that memory.

Beth is talking, but I'm not listening. That's okay because she's just trying to fill the emptiness to keep my mind off what's happened. But what I'm thinking about is her and how she might be able to save me. How it might be worth living after all, even without Craig and Mom, if I have her. But I have to be realistic. I'm just a freshman in high school and I probably won't spend the rest of my life with her. Sometime in the future, for some reason, we'll break up. But for now she is the best thing in my life and she's worth living for. And the fact that this feeling a person can give me exists is also enough. That I can love and be loved—I suppose that could be worth living for.

Eventually, Beth's mom knocks on the door and asks if I want a ride home. I say that I probably should go. My dad will be worrying.

Beth asks if I can stay a little longer, and her mom says, Well, I was going to go to bed soon.

Beth says she'll call Dawn and get a ride for us.

I wait alone in the room while she's making the call. I hear her on the phone and I hear Beth's mom and her boyfriend getting ready for bed, their voices muffled through the walls.

When it's almost time, Beth asks if I want to wait outside so she can smoke a cigarette. I say okay, and I go to the restroom. When I come back, she goes, and I quickly put on my coat. I zip it up and adjust it and try to make sure the gun is hidden. I can feel it pulling down the one side of the coat, but I look in the mirror and it looks discreet. I wish I hadn't brought it.

With the bruises on my face and the gray skin and black circles under my eyes, I look awful. I look how Dad looked under the fluorescent lights in the hospital. Broken. Sick.

Life changes. For worse sometimes. But sometimes for better. Like Beth would say, I have to wait. I have to hold on.

Outside, Beth goes through two cigarettes while we wait. We say almost nothing. Cold copper wires creep in under my coat to needle at my skin. The night is black, and our exhalations are so white and cloudy that there's almost no difference when Beth breathes out and when she blows cigarette smoke.

When Dawn's car pulls up, Beth tosses her cigarette and we walk to the curb to get in. Luke is with her, and as Beth and I climb in, he says, Hey, Danny, I'm so sorry about...

His voice breaks from holding back tears, and he doesn't finish.

Thanks, I say because I don't know what else to say.

Yeah, Danny, Dawn says, we're...

She trails off. We sit in silence for a minute with the car idling. It's warmer inside, but I can still see the faint trace of white in everyone's breath.

I just can't believe it, Luke says. I keep thinking that this can't really be happening.

Beth takes my hand in the backseat and sits close. She slides closer, but I shift away. I don't want her to brush up against the gun.

It feels like a bad dream, Dawn says.

They seem to want to talk about it with me, but it feels like Gretchen all over again. They want me to give them some catharsis, but I don't know why I need to be strong to help them get through this. I don't know what I owe anyone. And I don't understand why any of them think that how much they're hurting could compare with what I'm feeling.

Being with Beth today helped calm me, but I feel a tension in my shoulders now. I was able to put how terrible the world is out of my mind, but now all I can think about is Craig and how he's gone. He exists no more. He is less than the bursts of white breath from our mouths. He isn't even vapor.

Do you want to go home, Danny? Dawn says. Or do you want to go somewhere and hang out? I don't know, just to be around people. It's up to you.

A few minutes ago, I was ready to go home, to my room, and sleep. But I feel angry again. I don't want to go home. I don't want to pick Dad up off the couch and carry his passed-out body to his bedroom. I don't want to turn on *Headbangers Ball* or put on a cassette in my room. I don't want to walk into the house, expecting to see Craig and then remember that he isn't home. That he will never be home again.

Let's go to the river, I say. Let's build a fire and just...I don't know.

That's a good idea, Luke says.

There might be people there, Beth says.

If there are, we can leave.

I don't know how to say that I want to stare into a fire and not think. Just let numbness wash over me as I pretend, just for a little while, that this isn't my life.

Dawn drives, and the rest of us are quiet. The streets are empty. The drugstore's sign is off and the lights inside are dark. The Shell is lit up, but the pumps are vacant and its convenience store looks completely empty, with no one even behind the counter. The drive-through at McDonald's has no cars. A boy, alone, probably eleven or twelve, walks down the sidewalk on Main Street, his hands shoved into the pockets of his coat. I wonder who he is and what his life is like. He looks too young to be out by himself on a Saturday night.

On the road to the river, there are no streetlights. In the woods beyond the gray branches lies pure blackness. Dawn pulls onto the dirt road Craig and I drove down a week ago. The branches of the trees crowd in, clawing at the car. The tires crunch the frozen soil and puddles of ice.

There are a handful of cars in the clearing by the river, and seeing them there in a cluster makes me think of the previous week again, when I went here with Craig and we met up with Beth and the others. I feel like that happened years ago, not just days, and then the thought is there, fresh in my mind: Craig is dead. I forget it every few seconds, only for an instant, and then I'm reminded.

All of this is what I'm thinking about until the air in the car somehow changes, as if everyone is holding their breath, and I see what everyone else is seeing but not saying: one of the cars is Jamie Fergus's Camaro. I make out Jamie, leaning against his hood, his hands in his varsity jacket pockets, his head down as he talks to a group of three or four others.

We should go, Beth says.

Yeah, Luke agrees. Let's get out of here.

No, I say. It's okay.

My voice is calm, but my body is rioting. My heart. My breathing. My trembling limbs.

Danny, Beth says. I don't think that's a good idea.

It's okay, I say. I just want to talk to him.

Dawn parks ten feet from the nearest car. There are several people there, maybe ten, clustered around the fire barrel, their faces orange and ghoulish. Jamie stands on the other side of the barrel, leaning against the Camaro, glancing our way as he talks to the others. I don't think he can tell who is in the car yet.

He looks different somehow. He seems smaller, pulled in, as if he doesn't take up as much space as he used to. His nose is swollen from the fight, but the change in his face is more than that—he looks younger.

Let's just go, Beth says.

Her voice is frantic and high-pitched and doesn't even sound like her.

Nothing good can come of this, she says, almost in a shriek. Just drive away, Dawn!

No, I say.

I open the door and I stand, and Jamie sees me and a look comes over his face of shock and shame.

He stands up straight and looks around. He doesn't know what to do. It seems like the cruelest of jokes that this man, this boy, this less-than-human statue of meat and bones gets to go on living when Craig doesn't. There's not as much of a person there. There can't be.

I hate him because he simply gets to breathe. I hate him because the synapses still fire in his brain. The blood inside his body is still moving.

I walk toward him and unzip my coat.

Danny, he says, I'm sorry.

He doesn't try to make excuses or distribute blame. He simply says, I'm sorry.

He is earnest. He means it. I can see it in his face and in his body language. This is a new Jamie Fergus I have never seen before, transformed into a new creature. His face like a scared boy's, not the face of the man who has been terrorizing me.

The two of us are quiet, and everyone around us is quiet. It's as if we're in a bubble, and the rest of the world doesn't exist. Jamie and I are two celestial bodies, and everyone else is orbiting us in our own solar system, and he and I can't figure out which one of us is the sun and which one the planet. Our masses push and pull, and it feels like we were destined for this moment. Like each move that put us here—each argument, each taunt, each fight—was just part of machinery working. And somehow if one of us had done something different—if he and his friends hadn't beaten me up, if I hadn't said anything to Craig—then the machinery could have sputtered and stopped. But somehow we couldn't because it wasn't only us making the steps. We couldn't see the machine moving us to this moment, but the moment is here. And there is no way to stop the machine now.

What are you doing here? I say.

He looks down then looks up.

I just...I was going crazy in my house. I just had to get out.

I stare at him.

Danny, Beth says, we should go.

She reaches out and touches my arm, but I jerk it away and she recoils, startled at how violent my reflex is. I think about apologizing but I've gone through a transformation too and I don't care if I scared her.

Jamie opens his mouth, closes it, reopens it, and finally says, I just want you to know how sorry I am. I feel like this is all my fault.

It's not all your fault, I say. It's my fault.

No, he says, shaking his head. It's not.

It is, I say.

I reach into my coat and pull out the pistol in one slow, concentrated movement. Jamie's eyes widen. Someone gasps a few feet away. Beth or Dawn or both.

It's my fault, I say, because I should have just let Craig kill you.

Danny, Beth says. Don't.

I should have let him shoot Gretchen and then put the gun to your head like I'm going to.

Jamie tries to compose himself and stand strong. Even now he doesn't want to show fear. But the fear shows through anyway. His breathing comes out in fast, quick pumps. His eyes water. The firelight dances on his skin.

Danny! Beth says again, this time shouting it.

My heart is pounding, but the hand holding the Magnum is steady. I raise the gun. I point it at Jamie's face.

He inhales deeply and holds his breath, like death is a river he is about to jump into.

I cock the gun.

Beth steps in front of me, her forehead inches from the barrel.

I pull the gun down and hold it at my side and uncock it.

Jesus fucking Christ! I yell at her. Do you know what this thing can do?

People are backing away now, creeping down toward the river and up into the trees. I glance over Beth to Jamie and he sees me looking and he freezes.

You can't do this, Beth says. You can't, Danny.

Get out of the way, I say.

No.

I stare at her and she is beautiful—glowing—her eyes unflinching.

Get out of the way, Beth.

No, she says. You can't do this.

Heat emanates from the fire.

I move the gun and point it at the ground between us. The grip is cold.

Beth, I say. I love you.

She starts to cry. Her voice cracks as she says, I love you too, Danny.

Now get the fuck out of my way!

She shakes her head, crying hard now.

I look over her shoulder at Jamie. He is staring at me and I stare back.

I raise the gun and point it at Beth's face.

She winces and inhales, the noise like a leaking tire.

I cock the gun again.

Beth is sobbing but she won't move.

Don't take this from me, Beth.

This isn't the way, she says.

There is no other way.

There is.

He doesn't deserve to live!

But you do, she says.

I put my finger on the trigger. It's a hair trigger. A gentle squeeze and the bullet will go through her head. The barrel will rise an inch or two and I will feel the kick against my hand and I will hear the sound of the shot, but by then, it will already be over. Before she even sees the flame from the barrel, the bullet will punch through her skull, showering Jamie in her blood and brains and chips of skull. Her life—whatever life is—will go with it, exiting with the bullet and disappearing like it never existed.

The image of Mom's dead eyes comes into my mind.

I can't do that to Beth. And I realize—even with all that's happened—I can't do it to Jamie either. If I killed him, it would be like unplugging a machine. I would just turn him off. But I could never plug him back in. I could never turn him back on. There's no trigger you can pull to give life back. And Jamie, even Jamie, is a person, a world, a whole universe, someone as real as me.

I lower the gun.

I uncock it.

I drop my head.

Beth sobs loudly. Jamie is crying. Beth leans forward to try to hug me, but I step back and hold her away with my free arm.

No, I say.

Danny, she says, her eyes pleading. Give me the gun.

I look at her. How close I came to killing her.

I'm sorry, I say, and I turn and run.

I sprint toward the woods as fast as I can, the gun swinging heavy in my fist. Beth shouts for me to come back, but I lunge through the brush, stepping over logs, breaking through branches. When I'm far away, I stop at the riverbank and look out over the water and catch my breath. The surface of the river shimmers and writhes with a silvery hue on top of blackness, like the water is some kind of liquid metal machine. Besides my breath, the water is all I hear, the churning current and wavelets lapping at my feet.

I creep through the woods and follow a dry streambed. I find a corrugated metal culvert where the streambed goes under the highway. I crawl inside to hide and think. The bottom of the galvanized steel is caked with mud and branches and leaves. The air inside the culvert smells sour, like fruit that's gone bad. A car goes by overhead, and the sound echoes inside the culvert, a mechanical, filtered noise like talking into a fan. I imagine that the car is Dawn's and she and Beth and Luke are looking for me. Or Sergeant Frederickson's cruiser. I wait. The cold from the pipe seeps through my jeans and my coat. Time passes, and I think about what to do and finally I decide where to go.

I crawl out and uncoil my body, stretching in the dry ditch bed. A streetlamp glares down at me, and I see my shadow, dark black against the bright glow of the light. The barrel of the Magnum looks impossibly long in the shadow. I shove the gun inside my coat and climb out of the ditch. In front of me, I see two shadows, and I whirl to see who is behind. No one is there. Multiple streetlamps cast multiple versions of my own shadow. Several silhouettes—like images in a broken mirror—spread out around me. They could be different versions of me. Different futures.

When I make it to the cemetery, the sun hasn't risen yet, but the darkness is starting to fade. There is a hint of gray in the sky. The gravestones are all flat with the ground, simple marble markers with metal plates inscribed with names and dates. I know the way to Mom's grave well. The plaque, a bronze-tinted steel, says her name and the dates she lived. The marble is purplish-gray. I sat for hours last summer studying the designs in the stone.

I know she's gone. I know there's no heaven. She's not a ghost or an angel floating in the air around me. But still I talk to her like there might be something left of her in the universe. I don't speak the words, but I think them. I tell her that Craig is dead, and I tell her what happened, all the events leading up to it. I start to cry, and I cry so hard I fall onto my knees in the wet grass and hold my face in my hands.

I sit up. The sky is beginning to turn blue. I pull out the gun. Its stainless steel surface stands out silver-white in the dim light. I stare at it. I open the cylinder and see the six bullets loaded inside. I close the cylinder. I cock the gun. I uncock it. I hold it in both hands and feel the weight of it. I think about the weight of the world, my world, the one that exists in my head and exists around me. The world crushing me like a hydraulic machine that compacts trash or flattens cars. The weight of my life.

I think about all that has happened. Every action invites the events that follow, and I try to think about what I could have done—all the things I could have done—that would have put me in a different direction than the one I've been on.

But the river can't run backward.

Our fates might be preordained, written down somewhere or programmed like a machine. Numbers that come out to a certain solution no matter how much you add them up. Or maybe our fates are just accidents. Meaningless. Either way, it all feels out of my control.

But there is one thing I can control.

I hold the gun up to my head, touching the round tip against my temple. It's cold, like the chilled finger of a skeleton pressing into my skull. I pull the gun away and put it under my chin, pressing into the soft tissue.

This is just ceremony. I've always known that I would do it the way Mom did it, and so I take the gun and place the barrel between my teeth. The tip of the barrel presses into the roof of my mouth. With each breath, the steel of the gun fogs and then clears, fogs and then clears.

I put my thumb on the hammer to cock it back.

I close my eyes, and in the blackness, I search for something. My thoughts swirl around and mix and make no sense, not that I can see. Thoughts of Craig and Mom, Dad and Jamie and Gretchen, Sergeant Frederickson and Mr. James. Beth. Thoughts of creation and time and fate and pain. And what it means to live and what it means to die. I am just molecules and energy, and somehow the electricity in my brain makes me think I'm alive and that my happiness is something that's important.

I put my finger on the trigger.

I think of what my last thought should be. What do I want in my brain at the end?

Craig.

Riding in the car with him. The morning before he left.

I think of the two of us, gliding through the streets in the early morning light, patches of mist floating around us like clouds. Judas Priest on the stereo. If there is a heaven for me, this would be it.

I want to linger on the memory, enjoy it. But the memory moves on, and Craig and I are in the parking lot at school. The last time I saw him.

I love you, he says to me.

This time, in my mind, I can speak.

I love you too, I say.

Then don't do this, he says. I want you to live.

I shake my head and begin to cry.

I can't, I say. I can't do it without you.

The Nova is surrounded in a cloud of mist. There is no school. No reason for me to hurry to class. In this world, Craig and I have time. I know it's my imagination, and somewhere the real Danny is perched over a grave, a gun in his mouth. But it doesn't matter what's real and what's not.

Life is hard, he says. The bad gets mixed up with the good. Sometimes it will seem like there is more bad than good in the world. But the good, Danny, the good is worth enduring the bad for.

He goes on.

You're going to struggle with this your whole life. One day you might be happy, the next you might start thinking about killing yourself again. You have to decide to live. One day at a time.

Every day, you have to choose.

In the dream, I am crying and Craig is as he was that day in the car: sympathetic, serious, caring. The big brother watching over me.

I love you, Danny. I may be dead and I'm no angel and no ghost, but I still love you, and I will always love you. There may not be a god, but there is my love, and it will go on because it's inside of you. My love is as much a part of you as molecules and atoms, and just because you can't see it under a microscope doesn't mean it isn't there.

Live for me, Danny. Live for me when you can't find anything else to live for.

I cry and lean into him and hug him like I wish I had on the day he said good-bye. I love you, Craig.

I take the gun out of my mouth and lean over and put my face in the dead grass and cry. I sob and say it out loud: I love you.

When I'm empty and there's nothing left, I sit up and tilt my head back. I wipe my eyes and my nose. I breathe heavy frosty breaths in the cold air. The sky is bluer now. I see the glow of the sun from just below the horizon, orange and warm. I hear the hesitant chirp of birdsong.

I think of what Craig said. I know it was my mind giving Craig his words, but I think of them as his anyway. What he would say.

Every day, you have to choose.

I stare at the gun in my hands. I uncock it. I place it in the brown grass underneath Mom's grave marker. I lean forward and kiss the cold metal of her name. And then I stand, turn my back on the gun, and walk without its weight toward the warm sunrise.

I choose to live today.

NOTES & ACKNOWLEDGMENTS

An earlier version of the first chapter of this book appeared as a short story titled "Heavy Metal" in the *Jabberwock Review*. Thank you to Michael Kardos for publishing the story and making helpful suggestions even before I envisioned the story as a novel.

Thank you to William Lychack for selecting *Heavy Metal* for the Autumn House Fiction Prize and to Christine Stroud and the rest of the Autumn House Press staff for their hard work in bringing this book to print.

A big thank you to two superb writing teachers, Dan Chaon and Christopher Coake, and to two terrific mentors, Daniel Mueller and Evan Morgan Williams.

Several friends read earlier versions of this book, and I am grateful for the help they provided as I revised: Nancy Jackson, Edwin Lyngar, Michael Ryan, Jennifer Simpson, Samantha Tetangco, and Melanie Unruh. Their help was invaluable.

Thank you to my parents, Ron and Roberta Bourelle, who never discouraged me from doing what I love no matter how many unsettling stories I wrote.

Thank you to my brother, Ed Bourelle, not only for his help with the book but also for being my best friend. *Heavy Metal* is a book about brothers, and it could not exist without the love I have for mine.

And thank you to my amazing wife, Tiffany, and my extraordinary children, Ben and Aubrey. You make me happier than I ever knew I could be.

Andrew Bourelle has published short stories in *The Best American Mystery Stories, Hobart, Isthmus, Jabberwock Review, Kestrel, Prime Number Magazine, Thin Air, Weave, Whitefish Review*, and other journals and anthologies. *Heavy Metal*, winner of the 2016 Autumn House Fiction Prize, is his first novel. He lives in New Mexico with his wife and two children.

PREVIOUS WINNERS OF
The Autumn House Fiction Prize

Drift and Swerve	Samuel Ligon • 2008, selected by Sharon Dilworth
Attention Please Now	Matthew Pitt • 2009, selected by Sharon Dilworth
Peter Never Came	Ashley Cowger • 2010, selected by Sharon Dilworth
Favorite Monster	Sharma Shields • 2011, selected by Stewart O'Nan
What You Are Now Enjoying	Sarah Gerkensmeyer • 2012, selected by Stewart O'Nan
Come By Here: A Novella and Stories	Tom Noyes • 2013, selected by Kathleen George
Truth Poker	Mark Brazaitis • 2014, selected by Sharon Dilworth
Bull and Other Stories	Kathy Anderson • 2015, selected by Sharon Dilworth
Heavy Metal	Andrew Bourelle • 2016, selected by William Lychack

DESIGN & PRODUCTION

Text and cover design: Kinsley Stocum

This book is typeset in Calluna, a font designed in 2009 & published through the Dutch font fountry exljbris. The font was born by accident, but it was chosen for *Heavy Metal* very much on purpose.

This book was printed by McNaughton & Gunn on 55# Glatfelter Natural.